first french kiss *and other traumas*

first french kiss
and other traumas

Adam Bagdasarian

Melanie Kroupa Books
Farrar Straus Giroux
New York

Library of Congress Cataloging-in-Publication Data
Bagdasarian, Adam.
    First French kiss and other traumas / by Adam Bagdasarian.
        p.   cm.
    Summary: The author recounts humorous, sad, traumatic, romantic, and
confusing episodes from a fictional childhood.
    ISBN 0-374-32338-0
    I. Title.

PZ7.B14018 Fi 2002
[Fic]—dc21

                                                            2001050510

For my father
And my mother
And my sister
And my brother

contents

Dear Reader,

For many years my mother and brother had been after me to write a book of short stories about my childhood. I resisted writing the book because I considered myself a serious writer, and many of the stories were humorous, and I did not want to be a humorist. I wanted to be F. Scott Fitzgerald or Ernest Hemingway or James Joyce. I wanted to write the kind of important fiction that changes the world, and as far as I knew, not one important writer had ever written about summer camp or Little League.

So one day I sat down and began writing a very serious and consequential novel about a bartender in the style of F. Scott Fitzgerald, Ernest Hemingway, and James Joyce. The writing of this novel was such a trying and laborious process that I was convinced I was creating a masterpiece. But I wasn't. I was creating a trying and laborious novel that, in the end, was unreadable.

So once again my mother and my brother said, "Why don't you write those stories about your childhood?"

And this time I didn't argue. Maybe because the time was right, or because I was tired of being a plodding and painstaking writer and I saw this book as a chance to just be myself and have a good time. And I did have a good time. In fact, writing this book reminded me why I wanted to be a writer in the first place.

Though, so far, my life has occurred chronologically, my memories of it do not. Therefore, I invite you to join me on a random journey to the happy, confusing, humorous, traumatic, sad, romantic years of age five to age twenty.

My only regret is that I have only one childhood to write about.

Sincerely,

"Will"

first french kiss

I had been looking forward to the party for nine days. It was Maggie's party, and I liked Maggie, and, according to the notes she wrote me, she liked me too. In fact, according to her notes, she liked me first, Dale Koenig second, and Wayne Ratner third. I had been first ever since I lost my footing on the library stairs and slid headfirst across the hall floor into a wall. I had not seen anything particularly romantic about the episode, but when I regained consciousness in the nurse's office, there was a note in my pocket from Maggie saying that she hoped my head was all right and that she would like me more than anyone for the rest of her life.

This meant a great deal because Maggie Mann was the most desirable girl in the sixth grade. No one knew exactly why this was so, yet all a twelve-year-old boy had to do was stand next to her for five or ten seconds before he realized that subtle and mysterious forces were clouding his mind and making it impossible for him to breathe.

On the night of the party I combed and recombed my hair seven times before deciding that I had problem hair and would probably have to wear a hat for the rest of my life. I checked my face for blemishes and any sign of possible beard activity, gave up, slapped myself twice to bring the color to my cheeks, took a last look in the mirror, and decided that the overall impression, except for the hair, was just about perfect.

While my mother drove me to the party, the evening ahead appeared to me in a series of inspiring images. This, I knew, was going to be a memorable night: While the rest of my peers groped fruitlessly with their inhibitions, Maggie and I would be setting the emotional and romantic standards for generations of sixth graders to come. First we would dance, and then she would tell me she loved me or liked me a lot. "I didn't realize how much, until now," she would say.

"Nor I you," I would answer. Or something like that.

After my mother dropped me off, I slapped my cheeks once again, walked up the brick path that led to Maggie's front door, and rang the doorbell. Just before the door opened, I checked my zipper.

"Hello, William," Mrs. Mann said.

"Hello, Mrs. Mann," I said, wondering yet again how a girl as remarkable as Maggie could have a mother as matronly as Mrs. Mann.

"The party's in the living room," she said, leading me past a huge Japanese vase and a portrait of Mr. Mann.

When I entered the living room, I surveyed the scene derisively. As usual, the girls were on one side of the room talking and giggling in tight conspiratorial circles of three or four, while the boys stood on the other side comparing biceps, making fun of each other's clothes, and generally looking lost and uncomfortable.

The first person I looked for was Maggie. I saw her on the girls' side of the room talking with Kathy Colter and Joanne Lieberman. When Joanne saw me, she whispered in Maggie's ear, and Maggie turned, smiled, and began walking toward me. Because we had been communicating mostly by note for the last nine days and had not spent much time face-to-face, I found myself becoming a little nervous as she approached. I reminded myself that she was already mine and that there was nothing more to prove. This thought helped restore my pulse rate and blood pressure to almost normal.

"Hi," she said.

"Hi."

For a moment that was all I was able to say. Just the sight of her took my breath away.

"Have you tried the onion dip?" she asked.

"Not yet. Is it good?"

She nodded. "I made it."

I intended to say, "Well, if you made it, I know I'll like it," but it came out "Oh."

Just then, Joanne waved to Maggie across the room, made a face, and mouthed something.

"I think Joanne wants to talk to me," Maggie said.

"Okay," I said. Then, remembering that this was my

night and that I could do no wrong, I added, "Will you save the first slow dance for me?"

"Yes," Maggie said. I could tell by the way she said it that it was a special *yes*, but before I could savor my conquest, I was surrounded by friends and followers.

"Are you going to make out with Maggie?" Mike Dichter asked me.

"I may."

"Take her to the closet," Kevin Cox said. "That's where Eileen and I went."

"Which closet?"

"The one upstairs. For an hour."

An hour, I knew, was the record. I had set the first record of fifteen seconds the year before.

"When did you make out with Eileen for an hour?"

"Two weeks ago. You can ask her."

I had to wait fifteen minutes for the first slow song to play, and when it finally did, I walked over to Maggie as confidently as I had ever walked over to anyone, and said, "Would you like to dance?" She nodded, of course, and that nod assured me of so many things at once that I felt a little dizzy.

I walked with her across the floor, put my arm around her waist, took her right hand in my left, and began to melt. Never before had I held anyone so warm or so soft. Never before had a body conformed so perfectly to mine.

As we swayed gently in each other's arms, I realized

that we were the focus of every eye in the room, that every girl wished she was Maggie dancing with me, and every boy wished he was me dancing with Maggie. Halfway into the song, Maggie laid her head on my shoulder, and my head became light and all the colors in the room began to grow warm and dusky.

When the song ended, I looked at her. There was nothing to say, nothing to even try to say, so I smiled and she smiled and we separated to different parts of the party.

After my head cleared, I began to feel as confident and masterful as I had ever felt in my life. Maggie was mine—her face, hair, lips, arms, hands, voice, and magic were mine, and I felt as though I were hovering five or ten feet above the rest of my peers. Satisfied, I retired to a neutral corner of the room to bask in my well-being. Unfortunately, I was again surrounded by friends and followers.

"Why don't you ask her to make out?" Kevin asked me.

"I will when I'm ready."

"She wants to make out with you."

"How do you know?"

"Joanne told me."

"What did she say?"

"That Maggie wants to make out with Will."

Her opportunity came twenty minutes later when everyone formed a circle on the living room floor to play spin the bottle. I watched passively as each nonentity entered the circle and spun the bottle, knowing in my heart that there was only one boy, one girl, one spin, and one kiss that mattered.

When it was time for my spin, I took my place in the center of the circle and looked at Maggie. It was a smoldering, masterful look that caused every girl in the room to sigh and begin whispering. Then I gave the bottle a hard spin, watched as it made its only possible choice, and listened as everyone in the circle began to applaud.

Maggie stood, as though summoned by a sublime and irresistible fate, and floated across the floor toward me. We gazed at each other a moment, then kissed a lyrical, transportational kiss that astonished our friends, confounded our enemies, and silenced the room in general. Then, reluctantly, our lips parted and we returned to our places in the circle. Naturally, every spin of the bottle from that point on was irrelevant, and after three or four more spins, the circle broke up.

Now, I knew, my moment had come. The stage was set, my girl was waiting, and there was nothing for me to do but cross the twenty feet of floor that separated us, say something seductive, and take her away to some quiet private place. As I was walking toward her, she turned away from one of her friends and looked at me. At that moment everything about her seemed to say yes — "Yes, ask me," "Yes, I will," "Yes, you can," "Yes! Yes! Yes!" And so it was with a great deal of confidence that I faced her, put my hand on her shoulder, leaned toward her ear and whispered, "Do you want to make out?"

It sounded a little crude to me, but nevertheless she nodded.

As we were walking out of the room, I could feel the weight of four dozen eyes on my shoulders. I knew that everyone knew where we were going and that their hopes and expectations went with us. I also knew that I would not let them down. All I had to do was take Maggie in my arms, hold her face in my hands, press my lips to hers as hard as I could, and move my head from side to side until her knees got weak or she swooned or lifted one of her legs off the ground. I was not sure what scientific law made this lifting of the leg happen, but I had seen enough movies to know that it did happen and that it was going to happen to Maggie.

"In here," she said, opening the door to a bathroom.

When we walked inside, she turned on the light, closed the door, and put her arms around me. This, I knew, was my cue to turn off the light, take her face in my hands, and kiss her. So I turned off the light (plunging the room into absolute darkness), took what I hoped was her face in my hands, and pressed my lips against her chin.

"Wait," I said, turning on the light again. "I can't see too well." I studied her face for a moment, memorized the exact placement of her lips, turned off the light, and kissed her nose.

"I think you moved," I said, turning on the light again.

"I didn't move."

"Let's start kissing first, then I'll turn off the light."

Which is what we did.

After ten or fifteen seconds of kissing and making small noises of ecstasy, I realized that one of my nostrils was pressed against her cheek, the other against her nose. This meant that I couldn't breathe. I tried to find a way to kiss her and breathe at the same time, but no matter where I turned my head, her nose was always there. I didn't want to tell her this, of course, and interrupt the crescendo of passion I was certain we were building toward, so I continued kissing her and making small noises and moving my head back and forth. And now my face was beginning to get hot, as though I had a fever, and I knew that if I didn't breathe soon I was going to faint, so I opened my mouth, but instead of air I got her tongue.

I was so unprepared for this that my head moved back a little. I had never had another person's tongue in my mouth before and was not sure what I was supposed to do with it. I tried to make the best of things by putting my tongue in her mouth, but I didn't like the feeling, so I removed my tongue and concentrated on trying to suck air through the side of my mouth. This should have been a simple undertaking, but the more I pulled back in order to breathe, the more passionate and uninhibited she became, until my head was all the way back and hers was all the way forward and there was no telling who should be swooning and who should be feeling masterful.

Just before my lungs collapsed, I put my hands on

what would soon be her breasts, snapped my face away from hers, and turned on the light.

"What's wrong?" she said.

"I can't breathe," I said. "I'm sorry. Wait."

So she waited, and I inhaled and exhaled a few times, turned out the light, and kissed her nose again.

"Sorry," I said, turning on the light. "Let's kiss first."

So we kissed first, and I turned out the light, and before I knew it I couldn't breathe and her tongue was back in my mouth. I tried to push her tongue back into her mouth with *my* tongue, but she seemed to enjoy this and began making noises again, which I felt obligated to make with her.

Around this time I began to wonder how long we had been kissing. I knew I did not have a chance of breaking the record, but I wanted to make at least a respectable showing; so while we made noises together and turned our heads interminably from side to side, I determined how long ten minutes was in seconds and began my long count to six hundred. When I reached twenty-seven, I noticed that our cheeks were warm and wet. A moment later I realized that the wetness was drool and that it was coming from the side of my mouth that was sucking in air. At this point I had three choices: stop kissing Maggie, apologize, and go back to the party; turn my head yet another time and begin drooling on the other side of her cheek; or stay where I was, keep counting, and hope she didn't notice. I chose the latter, but by the time I reached two hundred and twenty-six, I could take no more, so I snapped my face away from hers, turned on the light, and said as pleasantly as I could, "Maybe we should go back to the party."

She looked at me for a moment with what might have been contempt, and nodded.

When we returned to the party, everyone looked a little surprised and disappointed. Maggie went to the girls' side of the room to tell her version of the story, and I went to the boys' side and fell back into a chair. Instantly, I was surrounded and everyone was asking me how it was. I might have said, "Wet, dark, suffocating, hot, and uncomfortable," but when I looked into their rapt, hopeful eyes, I knew I owed them something more, so with my last ounce of energy I grinned and said, "The best."

It was the least I could do.

life and times

I am born. I live in a neighborhood full of kids —a neighborhood of ponytails and crew cuts and women who bake bread and men who mow their lawns on Sunday.

My mother has green eyes and is compassionate and loving and susceptible to guilt. When I look at the sky at sunset, I see my mother.

My father is the disciplinarian. I can't put anything over on him. He seems to know what I am thinking before I think it. He has a smile that could warm a seventy-eight-room sixteenth-century stone Scottish castle in winter. He also has very definite limits, and a temper to guard them.

In school I fingerpaint and am forced to stand in a circle and do the hokey-pokey.

My friend Scotty and I eat raisins together and talk about frogs. We would both like to have frog legs so we can jump to China or Mexico.

One night my father comes home carrying three Grammys. One day he is being interviewed by a woman from Life *magazine. One night he tells my brother and sister and me about a house that has a staircase, a swimming pool, and a backyard bigger than our whole house:*

new house

Because my father was the only member of our family who genuinely liked change, he was the only one among us who was genuinely happy on the day we moved from our sweet yellow house in Van Nuys to the enormous stone mansion in Beverly Hills. My mother, who had resisted the move right up to the end, was solemn and edgy most of the day, and my brother and sister, who were leaving their school, their friends, their confidence, and their pride behind, seemed to be in a state of shock.

I was the second happiest member of our family, because, according to my father, the new house had a staircase, a banister, a swimming pool, a chandelier, and a basement. Also, I was only six years old and had no idea that I was leaving anything forever. As far as I was concerned, this was only a day of adventure—a day of moving men and vans and boxes and neighbors saying goodbye and looking sad for some reason.

The drive to the new house was a depressing experience. My father had gone ahead, so it was just my mother, brother, sister, and me. No one talked the whole way. No one even looked like they wanted to talk, so the only thing for me to do was look out the window and watch the familiar world gradually become unfamiliar.

When we got to the new house and went inside, I marveled at the wonderful green staircase and the chandeliers and the walk-in refrigerator and the backyard with its swimming pool and cabanas and carport. For the first half hour I felt as though I had come to a circus instead of a house, and its newness was an invitation to adventure and discovery. Of course, the front yard wasn't quite the same as our old front yard, and the neighborhood, with its clean silent streets and vaultlike mansions, did not seem as communal and inviting as our old neighborhood, but maybe it was, or would be soon. In the meantime I was meeting Eulalie, our new housekeeper, turning the chandeliers on and off, and watching the rainbows in the crystals.

Then my brother and I walked up the wonderful green stairs to our new bedroom, which was twice as big as our old bedroom and had pill-shaped pillows on the beds and marble sinks in the bathroom.

While my brother unpacked his clothes, I explored the rest of the house, turned the chandeliers on and off again, and ran up and down the stairs. On my third trip either up or down the stairs, I realized that something wasn't quite right. It was all new, of course, and exciting, but it was something else too—something that felt like cold space waiting to be filled—waiting to be warmed by experience and laughter and life. I tried to concentrate on the stairs and the banister and the chandeliers, but I could not help noticing that the green walls were not our walls, and that the green stairs seemed to recede to a vast unknown.

In defiance or self-defense, I went back upstairs to my room and talked to my brother as he hung up his clothes in his closet. For fifteen minutes we made happy faces and said happy words, but something was wrong—something that drew us into ourselves and made it impossible to talk in the old familiar way. I kept chattering about the banister and the walk-in refrigerator and the staircase, hoping that if I said enough happy things the feeling would go away, but it didn't, so we went outside to watch the moving men. As soon as we did, my brother said, "Hey, Will, we've got a tree." This meant that we had a climbing tree, which was good news because in Van Nuys we had had the best climbing tree in the world. It was thirteen or fourteen feet high, and every sturdy branch led right to the next branch until you reached the top, where two thick branches converged to make a very comfortable seat. I had noticed the tree a few hours earlier, when we first got to the house, and remembered thinking that it didn't look very good for climbing. Nevertheless, I now said, "Great!" in the hope that it would magically become a good climbing tree once we started climbing.

So we walked over to the tree, shinnied up the trunk to the first bough, climbed up, and sat there, five feet off the ground. My brother looked up to see if he could go any farther and discovered that the layout of the tree was such that he couldn't. Five feet was as much climbing as we were going to get in Beverly Hills, and it made my six-year-old heart sick, and my brother's ten-year-old heart four and a half years sicker. At that moment I knew why our neighbors had looked sad, and why my mother was edgy, and what goodbye meant. It meant sitting five feet off the ground in a strange tree with a heavy heart.

Neither my brother nor I said a word. We didn't have to. We just climbed down from the tree and went back to our room. I don't know exactly what was going through my brother's mind as he sat on his bed, but I'm sure it had something to do with feeling lost and forlorn and helpless and betrayed. I'm sure he was sifting through the rubble of his old life, pondering the speed with which he had fallen from extreme popularity to extreme obscurity. I, on the other hand, was bouncing back and forth between ecstasy and despair—one minute thinking about sliding down the banister, and the next about the green stairs receding to all that un-known. I don't know where my sister was, but I assume that she was in her room, either crying or trying not to cry. This, despite the fact that the walls of her room were painted a very pretty pink, and she had her own balcony.

Dusk came next, then dinner.

It was a nice dinner, mostly because my father could obliterate the strangeness of any house by the sheer force of his personality. Consequently, for the half hour that it took to eat, my brother and sister were their old selves, and we were once again a family sitting in a warm room eating dinner.

After each course my mother would press on a small mound under the carpet and a buzzer would buzz in the kitchen and Eulalie would clear our plates and serve us the next course. The novelty of the buzzer was enough to keep my mind occupied for most of the meal; and between that and my father's personality, no one stared sadly at their plate or lapsed into silence or started to cry.

After dinner, however, when my brother and I were back in our room, the old alien feeling of the house returned. Again, we tried to talk the way we had talked in the old house, but it still didn't feel the same, and finally there was nothing to do but get into our pajamas, turn off the light, close our eyes, and try to sleep.

If I had known then what I know now, I would have told my brother that in two years he was going to be the best athlete in school and be elected eighth-grade president. Then I would have gone to my sister's room and told her that her phone was never going to stop ringing and that she was going to be admired secretly and publicly by some of the most popular boys in her class. I would have told them both that we were home free—that nothing behind us would ever be lost, and everything ahead was going to be great.

But those years were still ahead, so all I could do was turn over on my side, look out the window at the new view, and listen to my brother toss back and forth under the covers.

my side of the story

I was sitting at my desk in my bedroom practicing my signature when my brother came in and asked me if I wanted to throw the ball around or shoot baskets.

"No," I said. So he looked over my shoulder at the signatures, went into the bathroom for a few seconds, came out, went to his own desk, unraveled an entire roll of Scotch tape and stuck it on my head.

Naturally, I was outraged. "What did you do that for?" I asked. It was a stupid question because I knew very well why he had done it. He had done it for the same reason he had stuffed me in the laundry hamper and tied me to a chair with my best ties. He had done it because he was fourteen and had the great good fortune to be blessed with a little brother he could bedevil at will.

"Try to get it off," he said.

This I attempted to do, but he had rubbed the Scotch tape so hard into my scalp that it had become a part of my head.

"Let me try," he said.

So he tried, and I yowled, and he stopped. Then he gently pulled a piece of the Scotch tape off the side of my head, along with six or seven of my temple hairs.

Even at the age of nine I knew that I had been mightily wronged; even at nine I knew that this violated every code of justice and fair play that I had ever been taught. And so, my heart full of righteous rage and indignation, I leaped out of my chair, past my brother, in search of justice.

In those days justice looked a good deal like my mother. It had lovely brown hair, a warm enchanting smile, and a soft, understanding voice. It was comforting to know that in a matter of seconds my mother would hear the evidence, weigh the evidence, and punish my brother. Generally, things were murkier. Generally, I did something by accident, then my brother did something back, and I did something back, and on and on until it was impossible to tell who was at fault. But this—this was the case of a lifetime. And the best part of all was that the evidence was stuck to my head.

When I reached my mother's room, I saw that the door was closed. For a moment I hesitated, wondering if she was sleeping; but I was so sure of my case, so convinced of the general rightness of my mission that I threw open the door and burst into the room screaming, "Mom! Mom! Skip put—"

And then I realized that I was talking to my father, not my mother.

In order to understand the enormity of the mistake I

had made, you have to understand my father. My father was five feet seven and a half inches tall, stocky, powerfully built, and larger than life in laughter, strength, character, integrity, humor, appetite, wit, intelligence, warmth, curiosity, generosity, magnetism, insight, and rage. Consequently, he was not concerned with the little things in life, such as sibling shenanigans, rivalries, or disputes. His job, as he saw it, was to make us the best human beings we could possibly be—to guide us, love us, and teach us the large laws of honor, courage, honesty, and self-reliance. He was the only man to turn to if you had a severed artery, broken ribs, or any serious disease or financial problems, but he was not the kind of man one would knowingly burst in upon screaming anything less than "The house is on fire!" or "Somebody stole your car!"

I knew this, of course, which is why I had run to my mother's room in the first place, and why, when I saw my father, most of the color drained from my face. My first impulse was to walk backward out of the room, closing the door gently before me as I did so, but I had shifted so suddenly from offensive indignation to defensive fear and astonishment that I felt a little disoriented. For a moment I considered telling him that I smelled smoke or saw someone stealing his car, but I couldn't lie. I couldn't tell the truth, either. In fact, for a moment, I couldn't speak.

"What the hell are you doing?" my father said.

I started to say, "I was sitting at my desk minding my own business, when—" and I stopped. I stopped because I knew instinctively that Scotch tape on my head was not enough, not nearly enough to warrant my wild, unannounced entrance into this room.

"When what?"

"Nothing."

"You ran in here screaming about something. What happened?"

"I didn't . . ."

"You didn't what?"

"I didn't know you were here."

"So what! You knew someone was here! What did Skip do?"

"Skip . . . uh. I was sitting at my desk, and Skip . . ."

"Skip what? Tell me!"

"Put Scotch tape on my head."

This apparently was all my father needed to set the wheels of his anger in motion.

"You came running in here without knocking because Skip put Scotch tape on your head?"

"No, I—"

"You didn't care that the door was closed? You didn't care that your mother might have been sleeping?"

I wanted to explain to him that this had been going on for years, that Mom and Skip and I had an understanding, but I knew that we weren't having a discussion. I also knew that he was working himself into a rage and that anything I said would only make it worse.

"Is that what you do? You run into rooms screaming?" He was on his feet now and advancing toward me. "You don't knock?"

"No. Yes."

At this point my brother entered the room, saw what was happening, and stood transfixed.

"Here!" my father said. "Here's what we do with Scotch tape!" And with that he pulled the whole wad off my head, along with fifty or sixty of my hairs.

I knew that he was only a few seconds away from his closing arguments now, and my calculations were just about right.

"You don't . . ." Whap! ". . . ever . . ." Whap! ". . . come in . . ." Whap! Whap! ". . . here . . ." Whap! ". . . without knocking! Do you hear me?" Silence. Whap! "Do you hear . . ."

At this point I heard a wheeze of escaping laughter where my brother was standing, and saw him run out of the room.

"Do you?"

"Yes, Pop, yes. I hear you."

"Are you ever going to come in here without knocking again?"

"No, no."

"Ever!"

"No."

"Now get out of here!"

And I got out and heard the door slam behind me.

———————

There was not much to do after that but sit at my desk and wonder what had happened. I had been signing my name, Skip put Scotch tape on my head, I ran to tell Mom, found Pop, and the lights went out. Where, I wondered, was the justice in that? Obviously, when I burst into my mother's room, I had entered a larger world of justice, a world where screaming, whining, mother dependence, not knocking on closed doors, and startling one's father were serious crimes. That part I understood. The part I didn't understand was the part about why my brother, who had started the whole thing by putting Scotch tape on my head, hadn't been punished. So, in the interest of a smaller justice, I went over to his trophy shelf, picked up one of his baseball trophies, and gradually wrested the little gold-plated athlete off its mount.

With a little luck, my brother would want to tell Pop about it.

the gum ball machine

I was lying on my bed, supposedly taking a nap, but I couldn't sleep—I couldn't even close my eyes. All I could think about was the gum ball machine that my father had gone out to buy for me. The whole idea of the machine was magical to me: the clear glass dome filled with shiny balls of gum, the slot for the penny, the silver handle, the turning of the handle—one hundred and fifty gum balls under the glass dome. It was a miracle, and soon, perhaps very soon, it would be mine.

Outside my window I saw a cloudy day—the kind of drab, colorless day that needed a gum ball machine to make it worthwhile. And the gum ball machine was coming, really coming! Soon I would be dropping the pennies, and turning the handle, and hearing the hard clink of the gum against the metal door. Soon I would be chewing the gum, and then . . . And then I would chew more gum, and more after that. And then . . . ?

And then? The question came so clearly, so persuasively that I sat up on my bed. Well, then I would chew it. But all it really was was gum, and I had chewed gum before a thousand times. Well, it was also the turning of the handle and the getting of the gum. So? I had turned gum machine handles before. So what? And somehow I could find no answer to that question, could find no reason on earth why a gum ball machine should matter at all; and I looked out my window at the cloudy day, and I could feel myself falling in that day, falling deep into the realization that there was nowhere to go, nothing to look forward to. It was only a gum ball machine; only a dome of glass, and a metal handle, and too much gum. And no matter how many times I turned the handle, all I would ever get was gum. And all I could ever do with the gum was chew it. Gum couldn't fly or talk or take me anywhere. It was just gum, and no matter how much gum I had, it would still be gum. And if there wasn't the gum ball machine, what was there? Days, that's what. Years and years of days. Days like balls of gum. Days of trees and sky and faces and food. The same trees, the same sky, the same faces, the same food. And the sameness enraged me because there was no escape from it, no alternative to it, nothing to do but sleep and submit. And the walls around me were of it, and my bed and glass windows were of it, and I could not break out. I would turn a handle and get gum; I would wake up and get a day; I would chew the gum; I would spend the day; I would spit out the gum; I would go to sleep. And all there would ever be for me were days and gum ball machines. No midnight magic carpet rides, no invisibility powders, no subterranean civilizations, no diamond men, no gold women, no talking dogs or dancing snails. Just gum balls under the glass dome, and days under the sky dome. Even Mexico, my imaginary retreat, would only be Mexico: another place of days, another trap of trees and water and food and faces; more of nothing, more of nowhere. And all the gum ball machines in the world couldn't change it because it was only gum and glass and metal. And I began to cry because I could not break the sky and go to Pluto, could not climb a tree and touch the moon, could not buy a carpet and fly away. I cried because there was nowhere to go and nothing to do—because my tears could not make a magic carpet, or an enchanted forest, or a genie, or a sprite. I cried because I thought that I was always going to be five years old in that static day waiting for a gum ball machine that didn't matter.

life and times

I am a decade old and cannot win a game of Monopoly to save my life. Every time I even come close to winning, my brother and my cousin band together, loan money to each other, give each other free passes when they land on the hotels, and pool their earnings to buy railroads. Soon I am broke, frustrated, and in jail.

I have lots of baby fat, which my brother sometimes grabs. My mother assures me that sometime soon I will lose the baby fat and grow into my ears, which are large by most standards. My brother calls me Dumbo. I laugh because I have absolutely no vanity. As proof of this, I continue to have my hair cut at Dan's Snip and Curl. Dan cuts my hair, then lacquers it so that it will not move in a tornado. My lacquered hair feels like hard plastic and can be snapped off in pieces and examined.

Although gregarious and extroverted, I have a very definite private world. In this world I am a secret agent, a star athlete, a ladies' man. I move like a cat and have catlike reflexes. However, after watching Damn Yankees *eight times* in one week on *The Million Dollar Movie,* I develop a crush on Gwen Verdon and begin to move less like a cat and more like a dancer.

If I were asked to make a list of the top five things I would like to do during summer vacation, I would start with reading comic books. After that would come lighting firecrackers, eating chocolate cake, sleeping at the Finley household, and going to Seattle for the World's Fair. But my father has made his own list of the top five things he would like me to do during summer vacation. And his list starts with camp:

mount cinder

It certainly wasn't camp the way we thought camp should be. Camp, we assumed, was dinner in mess halls, fruit punch, corn on the cob, baseball, badminton, rope climbing, and cool walks through the forest. Camp, as far as we knew, was not a black sand mountain called Mount Cinder in ninety-five-degree heat with twenty-five-pound packs on our backs and a burning sun overhead. Camp, we had heard, was supposed to be fun.

"It'll be good for you," our counselor, a red, round-faced, sturdy-looking man named Russ, said. "And I promise you when it's over and you're standing on top of that mountain, you're gonna feel great."

He went on to say that the mountain was not really a mountain but a goal, and if we backed down from the mountain, we would spend the rest of our lives backing down from things.

Then he said, "Let's go."

Despite our misgivings we were a pretty cheerful lot

at first, singing and whistling and generally enjoying the sensation of the smooth sand beneath our heavy boots. Thirty or forty yards later, however, the whistling died down and the voices grew faint and there was only the hot silence, pierced occasionally by small wheezes and groans.

"Don't look up," Russ said. "Just keep your eyes on the sand in front of you. One step at a time."

Step by heavy step we labored, our legs sore, our mouths dry, our heads down. The heat was fantastic. Not just a regular summer heat but a searing, bullying heat that sapped not only our energy but our spirits as well.

Fifteen minutes later the groans were louder, and half of our number were complaining of dizziness, sore feet, and strap burns.

"Are we really going to feel different after we reach the top?" I asked.

"You bet," Russ said.

Five minutes later I said, "What if we back down from the mountain this time, and then next year we all come back and climb it?"

"You'll never make it," Russ said. "If you back down once, you back down forever. You can't cheat the mountain."

So I kept my head down and noticed that for every step I took, I slid back a half step in the sand. When I mentioned this to Russ, he said, "That's life. Two steps forward, one step back."

Actually, I didn't want to go to camp in the first

place, but my father was concerned about my character and had convinced himself that, given a choice, I would rather sit on my mother's lap than drive a tractor, which, in fact, was true—if those were the only two choices I had.

"He's going to camp," he told my mother one night, and two weeks later a black-haired, hearty-looking man who called himself Uncle Bob was sitting in our living room showing us a film about Camp Bob. The film showed happy, clean-cut youths, not unlike myself, smiling at the sky, breathing deeply, and petting horses.

According to Uncle Bob, Camp Bob provided everything a healthy, well-adjusted boy or girl could want out of life: good food, archery, swimming, camp songs, and companionship.

"Where do the boys sleep?" my father asked. I could tell he liked Uncle Bob immensely and that I was going to camp no matter where "the boys" slept.

"In A-frames," Uncle Bob replied. "Brand-new, oak wood A-frames. No carpet, of course," he chuckled, "but plenty of comfort for a boy."

As it turned out, the only one who slept in an A-frame was Uncle Bob, and it had plenty of carpet, as well as two television sets, an elaborate alarm system, and a jacuzzi. *We* slept in small square windowless shacks with warped wood floors and red ants.

"Kids love Camp Bob," Uncle Bob told my mother and father. Then he told them about his enthusiastic and reliable staff, smiled, and left the house with a signed check from my father.

"How about a song?" Russ said, jarring me out of my reverie. And then he began to sing: "A hundred bottles of beer on the wall, a hundred bottles of beer. If one of those bottles should happen to fall, ninety-nine bottles of beer on the wall. Ninety-nine bottles of beer on the wall, ninety-nine bottles . . ."

He went on like that, alone, until there were only fifteen bottles of beer on the wall and Joey Becker rolled ten feet down the mountain.

"Hey!" someone shouted.

"Hold it up," Russ said, turning around. "Someone get Joey."

We all looked at one another. Although most of us liked Joey, none of us wanted to lose ten feet to retrieve him.

"Why don't we just come back for him later?" someone asked.

"The last man in line gets Joey," Russ said. "That's you, Dirk."

Dirk, despite the promise of his name, was perhaps the frailest member of our group. He had come to camp with a typed list of his infirmities, along with a few dietary do's and don'ts. To the best of our knowledge he suffered from soft bones, sensitive teeth, sinusitis, and homesickness; he was afraid of water, insects, horses, bright lights, no lights, and closets. Nevertheless, he started down the hill for Joey.

"How is he?" Russ called to him.

"He's . . ."

Dead, I thought.

". . . okay," Dirk said. "But he says he can't go on."

"Help him up," Russ said.

Dirk tried to help Joey up, then looked at Russ. "He says if I touch him, he's going to hit me."

"He's not going to hit anybody," Russ said, "because he knows if he does, he's going to have to hit me too."

Dirk tried one more time to help Joey to his feet, and this time Joey let him.

"How do you feel, Joey?" Russ called.

Joey, who seemed too weak to answer in words, nodded once, sullenly, and slowly joined the rest of us.

"Let's go," Russ said. "Just three hundred more yards."

After only twenty of those yards, the groans and wheezes began again along with pleas to stop, pleas to slow down, and pleas to turn back.

For some reason, Russ thought that this was the perfect time to tell me all about himself. He had three brothers and two sisters. His oldest sister's name was Anne. Penny, the youngest, played piano. His three brothers were forest rangers, each for a different forest. He told me that everyone is allotted a certain number of heartbeats at birth and that people who smoke or gamble use up their heartbeats faster than people who don't. His goal, he said, was to lower his heart rate down to ten or fifteen beats a minute, which meant that he might live to be a hundred and thirty or a hundred and thirty-five years old.

At this point I stopped listening, not because I was bored but because I realized that if what he had said about heartbeats was true, then at the rate my own heart was beating, I had already used up my childhood and young-adult years and was rapidly closing in on middle age.

And then Russ's voice began to sound like a waterfall, and I knew I was going to die.

"Only sixty more yards," he said.

Whoosh, I heard.

The cries of my comrades were no longer the cries of boys but of seagulls, and the sand before me sparkled first like diamonds, then like the sea.

Just as I was about to close my eyes and surrender to that sea, I felt a surge of strength and determination inside me that demanded not only that I stop hallucinating but also that I make it to the top of the mountain on my own two feet. I do not know if it had something to do with achieving goals or facing life, but for some reason I knew that I wanted to make it—I *had* to make it, I was determined to make it. Even if I never did another worthwhile thing for the rest of my life, even if the rest of my life only amounted to five or six more minutes.

"Thirty more yards," Russ said.

I had never before felt such strength inside myself, and nothing, not my heavy boots or my twenty-five-pound backpack or my aching legs, was going to stop me. *Head down*, I thought. *One step at a time.*

"Twenty more yards," Russ said.

Every step, I knew, was building up my character,

and by the time I reached the top of the mountain, I would have so much character that I would be almost unrecognizable.

"Ten more yards."

I conquered those last ten yards, and then, miraculously, it was over. I had faced the mountain, met the challenge, achieved the goal. I stood very still for a minute, waiting for a wave of superiority or masculinity to wash over me.

"Well, you made it," Russ said. "How do you feel?"

"Okay," I said. "When do I start to feel great?"

"Sometimes it takes a little time to sink in," Russ said.

So I sat down near a big rock and gave it time to sink in. After five minutes I felt like exactly the same person I had been before I climbed the mountain, only thinner and less cheerful. By this time my fellow campers were slumped here and there beside me, and I asked Joey Becker if I looked different.

"I can't breathe," he said.

"But do I look different to you, Joey?" I asked, clenching my teeth a little to make my jaw stand out.

"You look the same," he said. "Leave me alone."

So I got up and walked around for a little while and tried to *feel* different. I looked at the mountain I had just climbed and tried to love it or disdain it or feel at one with it or superior to it, but it just wasn't in me.

Dejectedly, I walked back to my rock and pondered the situation. I had trusted my counselor, climbed the mountain, met the challenge, and gained absolutely nothing. I did not feel a foot taller or twenty years wiser or even better looking. I felt exactly like myself only . . . only better. Only a little bit better.

"Everybody up," Russ said. "It's two miles to Horseshoe Lake."

little league

In Little League my brother was a .500 hitter, an all-star, a natural-born competitor, a coach's dream.

I am what the coach sees when he wakes up. I cannot run, hit, field, catch, or throw and am sent to the Siberia of the baseball world—right field. Very few balls are ever hit to me in right field. When I see a ball sailing toward me, a flashbulb explodes in my head and my knees begin to shake. As the ball begins its descent, I try to remember everything I ever learned about baseball. Nearing hysteria, I open my mitt wide and hope for the best. Then I hear the ball plop three feet to my left and the angry voices of my teammates exhorting me to pick up the ball and throw it. I see them all waiting while the enemy rounds the bases. Frantically, I run to the ball, trip over a sprinkler head, regain my balance, pick up the ball, and throw. There are six open mitts for the ball to go into, but it sails over all of them and into the fence. The runner scores. My coach rolls his eyes. The game is lost.

When I come up to bat two days later, I am told to just make contact. I am also reminded by three-fourths of the team that a walk is as good as a hit. As I step into the batter's box, all the tautness goes out of the players on the opposing team: the third baseman examines his glove; the first baseman puts one hand on his hip; the shortstop yawns; the second baseman stands to his full height and waves to his mother; the outfielders move in fifteen feet and begin recreasing the bills of their baseball caps. I am humiliated in the extreme and would like nothing better than to hit a line drive down the middle, but I know that I won't.

The first pitch whizzes by me so fast that I do not have time to get the bat off my shoulder.

"Get the bat off your shoulder!" someone yells from the stands.

The next pitch is a ball, but I swing anyway.

"Good eye, good eye," the opposing team taunts sarcastically.

I foul the next pitch off, so the count is still oh and two. I want to hit a home run so bad, I can taste it. The pitcher and I look each other in the eye. We both smile. I go into my batter's crouch and await the next pitch. It is a fastball that hits me on the leg. My teammates cheer as though I have done something remarkable. I hobble to first base and am immediately taken out for a pinch runner.

In the next three weeks, I lose two flyballs in the sun, strike out four times, and am tagged out at second base. For this reason I am generally happiest sitting on the bench and working on the creases in the bill of my baseball cap. The assistant coach tells me that I just need a little experience. He tells me to keep my eye on the ball at all times. I tell him about the sprinkler in right field, and he nods his head. I don't think he believes me, so I offer to show it to him. He says we are getting off the point. He says the point is for me to keep my eye on the ball at all times. When the ice-cream truck comes, he gives me a dollar and asks me to get him a drumstick and a snow cone.

At the end of the season my mother tells me it's only a game. Many great men, she says, were never good athletes.

Nine months come and go. During that time my brother teaches me how to hit and field. I also grow an inch and feel more coordinated. It is like magic. What is even more magical is that one month into the new Little League season, I am hitting .400 and am considered one of the best players around. My coach talks to me often, tells me his first name, introduces me to his wife and children, puts his arm around me, and tells me that I am his boy. As his boy, my job is to get two hits a game, dig bad throws out of the dirt, and help him win the pennant. I tell my coach that I do not like his wife and will quit the team if she ever comes to another home game. Instantly, my coach informs the guard at the gate that his wife is now *persona non grata*. Still in a huff, I talk to the press and tell them I don't like having to sit on the same bench with players who are only hitting .300. I get a bad reputation and am traded to

Cleveland for a relief pitcher and a minor league catcher. In Cleveland I begin dating heavily and am traded to Houston. In Houston I take a vow of chastity and win the batting crown.

I am twelve years old now and facing mandatory retirement. Rather than fight the system, I choose to step down quietly. It's good to be back in the sixth grade.

popularity

Somewhere inside me I knew that ten-year-old boys were not supposed to spend their recess circling oak trees in search of four-leaf clovers. Still, that's what I and my equally unpopular acquaintances, Allan Gold and Allan Shipman, were doing while the rest of our classmates played tag and kickball and pushed each other higher and higher on the swings.

Aside from having a little more than our share of baby fat, the two Allans and I had very little in common. In fact, we could barely stand one another. Still, during recess we were the only company we had, so we tried to make the best of it. Now and then one of us would bend forward, pick a clover, examine it, shake his head, and let it fall to the ground.

"Got one," Allan Gold said.

"Let's see," Allan Shipman said.

Allan showed Allan the clover.

"That's only three."

"No, that's four. Right here. See?"

"That's not a whole leaf," Allan Shipman said sourly. "There's one leaf, two leafs, three leafs."

"Four leafs!"

"That's not a whole leaf!"

We had been looking for four-leaf clovers every school day for six months. And each of us knew exactly what he would do if he ever found one: he would hold the lucky clover tight in his hand, close his eyes, and wish he was so popular that he would never have to spend time with the other two again.

"Got one!" Allan Shipman said.

Allan Gold swiped the clover from him. "One, two, three," he said, throwing it to the ground.

"There's four there! That was a four-leaf clover! Pick it up!"

"You pick it up!"

"You pick it up!"

"You!"

"You!"

While the two Allans faced off, I looked across the black tar and asphalt at a crowd of boys who were making more noise and seemed to be having more fun than anyone else on the playground. These were the popular boys, and in the center of this group stood their leader, Sean Owens.

Sean Owens was the best student in the fourth grade. He was also one of the humblest, handsomest, strongest, fastest, most clear-thinking ten-year-olds that God ever placed on the face of the earth. Sean Owens could run the fifty-yard dash in six seconds, hit a baseball two hundred feet, and throw a football forty yards. The only thing Sean didn't have was a personality. He didn't need one. When you can hit a baseball two hundred feet, all you have to do is round the bases and wait for the world's adulation.

I gazed at Sean and the rest of the popular boys in bewildered admiration. It seemed like only yesterday that we had all played kickball, dodgeball, and basketball together; and then one morning I awoke to find that this happy democracy had devolved into a monarchy of kings and queens, dukes and duchesses, lords and ladies. It did not take a genius to know that, upon the continent of this playground, the two Allans and I were stableboys.

I had been resigned to my rank for many months, but now, looking at the two Allans (still arguing over the same three-leaf clover), then at the popular boys, I suddenly knew that I could not stand another day at the bottom—I wanted to be a part of the noise and the laughter; I wanted, I *needed*, to be popular.

Being ten years old, I did not question this ambition, but I did wonder how on earth I was going to realize it. Though I only stood twenty yards from the heart of the kingdom, I felt a thousand miles removed from the rank and prestige of its citizens. How could I bridge such a gap, knowing I might be stared at, or laughed at, or belittled to a speck so small that I could no longer be seen by the naked eye? And as I stood on that playground, torn between fear and ambition, those twenty yards began to recede from view, and I knew that I must either step forward now, or retreat forever to a life of bitter companions and three-leaf clovers.

I took a deep breath and then, with great trepidation, crossed the twenty longest yards I had ever walked in my life and found myself standing a few feet from the outer circle of what I hoped was my destiny. I lowered my head a little, so as not to draw attention to myself, and watched and listened.

Mitch Brockman, a lean, long-faced comic, considered by many to be the funniest boy in the fourth grade, was in the middle of a story that had something to do with Tijuana and a wiener mobile. I wasn't sure what the story was about, but there was a lot of body English and innuendo, all of which the crowd seemed to find absolutely hilarious.

I noticed that every time Mitch said something funny, he eyed Sean Owens to see if he was laughing. He was. Silently. His mouth was open, but it was the laughter of the other boys that filled the silence. I realized then that Mitch was Sean's jester. As long as he could make Sean laugh, he was assured a prominent position in the group.

I wondered what *my* position in the group might be. I certainly wasn't a great athlete, student, or ladies' man, but I did have a sense of humor. Maybe I could be the *second*-funniest boy in the fourth grade. My thoughts went no further because the bell ending recess rang. But that night, just before I fell asleep, I saw myself standing in the center of the popular boys telling the funniest stories anyone had ever heard. I saw Sean Owens doubled up with laughter. I saw myself triumphant.

I returned to the group every recess, for three days. I stood, unnoticed, just outside the outer circle, waiting for my moment, for the one joke or wisecrack that would make me popular. I knew that I would only get one chance to prove myself, and that if I failed, I would be sent back to the stables. And so, with the single-mindedness of a scientist, I listened to the jokes the other boys made, hoping to align my comic sensibilities with theirs. Now and then I found myself on the verge of saying something, but every time I opened my mouth to speak, Mitch would launch into another routine, and my moment passed, and I had to resign myself to yet another day in the dark.

I did not know then that popularity has a life span, and that Mitch's time was about to run out.

It is a sad fact of life that the clothes a child wears and how he wears them often determine his rank in school society. I knew it, Sean Owens knew it, everyone in school knew it. So maybe it was carelessness, or temporary insanity, or a subconscious desire to step back into the stress-free shadows of anonymity that caused Mitch Brockman to wear a yellow shirt with a yellow pair of pants. He might have gotten away with it if I hadn't left for school that same morning unaware that one folded cuff of my jeans was noticeably lower than the other. As it was, the two of us were on a collision course that only one of us would survive.

At recess on that fateful day, I took my customary place a foot from the popular boys (wondering if I would ever get a chance to prove myself) and listened to Mitch tell another variation of his story about the wiener mobile. I pretended to enjoy this story as much as the others, while my mind strayed to a dream world where I did not have to feel so out of place, and Mitch and Sean and I were the best of friends. And then, with a suddenness that jarred me back to reality, Mitch Brockman, a boy who had never noticed me, never seemed to know or care that I was alive, turned to me, pointed at my uneven pants, and said, "Someone needs a ruler."

This was, perhaps, the wittiest remark he had ever made, and I froze. With four words he had devastated all my aspirations, defined me as a fool, and all but condemned me to a life of shame and obscurity. I could see my future, my boyhood itself, crumbling to dust, and as I heard the laughter and felt the heat of the spotlight upon me, I pointed at Mitch's yellow pants and shirt and said, "Someone else needs a mirror. You look like a canary." Then, with the grace of a magician's assistant, I raised my left arm in a presentational gesture and said, "Boys, I give you Tweety Bird."

And it was all over. As the volume of the laughter doubled, Mitch seemed to vanish, and that day, on that playground, Sean Owens's laughter was heard for the first time. In an instant, Mitch Brockman became Tweety Bird, and I, an absolute nonentity, became somebody. And then somebody special. Someone to seek out. Someone to follow. Sean Owens's first jester and best friend. The entire transformation was complete in a matter of months.

During this time Mitch became a less and less vocal part of the group, telling fewer and fewer stories, until finally, the following year, he was gone—to another school perhaps, or another state, or another country. I never knew. No one knew because no one noticed—no one had called him for months. But *my* phone rang. *My* weekends were filled with sleep-overs and baseball games and bowling parties and bicycle races and more new friends than I knew what to do with.

And I did not trust one of them, because I knew then that I was standing on sand and was only a yellow shirt and pair of pants away from the oak trees where the two Allans were still looking for four-leaf clovers.

going steady

Linda Lieban was an artist, a free spirit, a bohemian who played the flute in the park, drew pictures of winged horses and naked nymphs, and signed these drawings with the blood from her own pricked finger. She was someone, we all knew, who was destined to go to New York, dance on tabletops, pose naked for struggling artists, and rally the masses to riot.

One day, for some reason, she smiled at me in art class. After I passed her a note asking her why, she passed me a note saying that I knew why, and I passed her a note saying that I really didn't, and she passed me a note telling me to guess, and I passed her a note asking if she liked me, and she passed me a note with a heart on it that said "Yes!"

So Linda Lieban, one of the prettiest girls in the seventh grade, liked me. I was immensely proud of my conquest, though I had no intention of doing anything about it, partly because she frightened me and partly because, in those days, it was my ambition to collect as many female hearts as possible without committing my own heart to any particular one.

Unfortunately, during recess Greg Ransohoff mentioned that he had a crush on Linda, and I mentioned that I could go steady with her anytime I wanted.

"Oh sure," he said.

"Wanna bet?" I said.

"How much?"

"A dollar."

"Okay," he said, "there's Linda. Go and ask her."

So I walked over to Linda and asked her to go steady with me. She said yes, of course, but before she could kiss me or embrace me or hold my hand, I walked back to Greg Ransohoff and said, "She said yes. Give me a dollar."

So now I was going steady with Linda Lieban, which meant that I would have to call her every night, gaze at her during class, stop flirting with other girls, write romantic letters signed with a heart, carry her books, defend her if necessary, and generally stop being myself. Also, Linda was a girl who, though lovely, was looking for someone to love much as a boa constrictor looks for a small pig or owl to swallow.

That night I called her and did my best to sound as docile and love-struck as possible. This I accomplished by lowering my voice an octave and whispering as though I had laryngitis. A half hour into our conversation she asked me if I loved her, and I said, "Of course," and she said, "How much?" and I said, "A lot," and she said, "I love you more," and I said, "No, you don't," and she said, "Yes, I do," and I said, "No, you don't," and she giggled and I giggled and she hung up and I felt a little queasy.

The next morning during recess she walked over to me coyly with her hands behind her back, kissed me, said, "Hi, lover," and handed me a small white stuffed unicorn with silver glitter on its horn, its tail, its mane, and its hooves. She handed it to me as though it were a baseball signed by Willie Mays, and I took it as though it were a poison apple.

"Do you know what it means?" she asked.

"No," I said, which was the first honest thing I had said to her since I asked her to go steady.

"It means I love you."

"Oh," I said, trying to look grateful and moved. Then the bell ending recess rang and she kissed me and we walked together arm in arm toward our next class.

During math class she handed me a note covered with red hearts and when I looked at her she blew me a kiss and I managed to smile and kiss the air and Mrs. Fine said, "William, if you are going to carry on with your girlfriend, you can do it in the vice-principal's office."

Naturally, we talked on the phone that night:

"Hi, lover," she said.

"Hi," I said in my breathy baritone.

"Do you miss me?"

"Yes."

"Come over."

"Now?"

"Right now."

"It's nine o'clock at night, Linda."

"So? Sneak out."

"I can't sneak out."

"Sneak out now and throw a pebble at my window."
I laughed nervously.

"Then *I'll* sneak out and throw a pebble at *your* window," she said.

Here was the Linda I had feared. Here was the bohemian, free-spirited Linda who would come to my house, throw a pebble at my window, alarm my parents, and ruin my life.

"No, no," I said. "Let's just go to sleep instead and *think* about each other."

"I'm thinking about you now!"

"It's different when you're in bed. Pretend we're lying under the stars together."

"In Oregon?"

"Okay, Oregon."

"I love you, lover," she said.

"I love you, too," I said.

"Not as much as I love you."

"Yes, I do."

"No, you don't."

"Yes, I do."

"No, you don't."

Then she giggled and I giggled and she hung up and I felt queasy again.

Things proceeded in roughly this fashion for four days. By the end of the fourth day I knew I had to break up with her. I was tired of cooing, kissing the air, and carrying her books. I was tired of looking love-struck and docile and content. Also, I knew that one night she really would throw a pebble at my window, and if I pretended to be asleep, she would throw a rock, and Sam, our dog, would bark, and my parents would wake up, and all hell would break loose.

On Friday she asked me if I was going to Chris Block's party Saturday night.

"I didn't even know he was having a party," I said.

"He sent our invitation to my house."

"*Our* invitation?"

"Uh-huh."

That night I decided I would break up with her at Chris Block's party. "Linda," I said to the mirror, "it's not working. We're two different people looking for two different things.

"Linda," I said, "sometimes two people, even if they love each other, can't be together.

"Linda," I said, "let's break up . . . I think it's time to break up . . . let's do ourselves a favor and break up."

And no matter what I said, my imaginary Linda smiled, told me she understood, and walked cheerfully out of my life.

The night of the party I felt happier than I had felt for a week. I decided that I would not waste any time. As soon as I got to the party, I would pull Linda aside, explain the situation as tenderly as I could, kiss her on the cheek, and enjoy my freedom.

Unfortunately, it didn't quite work out that way because as soon as I got to the party, Linda ran over to me, picked a piece of lint off my jacket, told me I looked delicious and that she had missed me all day. As I started to say, "Linda, sometimes two people, even if they—" she said, "Come on," led me into Chris Block's living room where everyone was dancing, and said, "Let's dance."

So we danced. To be absolutely honest, she felt very good in my arms, and for one brief moment I was actually happy that she was mine. When the song ended, however, I remembered that I had to reclaim my freedom and said, "Linda, I have to talk to you." With that, I led her out to the backyard, past a row of rosebushes, to the swimming pool. I sat her down on the diving board, took a deep breath, and looked at her.

"Linda," I began. "Lover . . ." She smiled. "I . . . I have something to say."

She looked earnestly into my eyes.

"I love you," I said.

"I love you too. Is that what you wanted to tell me?"

"Yes," I said. "That's all. Let's go back to the party."

"Did you buy the ring?"

I had promised to buy her a ring.

"I ordered it," I said. "Yes."

"What kind of ring?"

"Gold," I said.

Linda smiled, stood up, and kissed me. Then we went back to the party. Ten minutes later, after one slow dance, a glass of punch, and endless cooing and pet name calling, I asked her to come outside with me again. I was determined to succeed this time, determined to sit her down, speak my piece, and regain my freedom. So I took her by the hand, walked her back to the diving board, sat her down, and after a few false starts, told her I loved her again and walked her back to the party.

This, I knew, could not go on. A real man, I knew, could look a girl in the eye, speak his piece, and walk away. A real man was nobody's puppet, nobody's property. I simply had to take her outside again, sit her down, and get it over with.

So I walked over to her, looked her in the eye, and said, "I have to talk to you."

"Again?"

"It's about the ring," I said.

So once again we walked out to the backyard, past the rosebushes to the diving board.

"Linda," I said, "how do you feel?"

"Fine," she said.

"Happy?"

"Yes."

"Are you sure?"

"What do you mean?"

"Don't you sort of feel like something isn't right—like maybe you could be happier, or *I* could be happier?"

Here her face changed. I was about to tell her that I loved her again and take her back to the party, but I knew that this was my last chance to prove to myself that I had character and backbone.

"No," she said. "Do you?"

"I think so," I said. And then, because that sounded too spineless and weak-willed, I added, "Yes. Yes, I do. I want to break up."

I had prepared myself for at least a dozen questions, but she did not say a word. She just looked at me. Then her eyes filled with tears and she ran back to the party.

I would like to say that I ran after her, but I didn't. I would like to say that I held her in my arms and comforted her until she stopped crying, but I didn't do that either. I would like to say that we parted that night with a warm and enduring understanding of each other, and that we remain good friends to this day, but we didn't and we aren't.

What I did do was watch her run into the house. Then I smiled. I smiled because I had stood my ground—because I had had the strength and character to look a girl in the eye and break up with her. So proud was I of my achievement, so sure was I of my irresistible attraction to women, that ten minutes later I went back to the party, found Eileen Weitzman, and asked her to go steady.

time

He had always known about time. Time, they said, flies. Time comes and time goes. Time waits for no one. And sure enough he was no longer in the first grade and he knew how to read and he liked girls and he couldn't quite imitate his sister's voice on the phone anymore. That part he liked.

The part he didn't like, as he lay in bed one October night, was the part about his brother. Time was going to send his brother to college, away from home, away from this room, away from their life together. Sooner or later time was going to give his brother two suitcases and a plane ticket and send him far away. It did not matter that his brother was sixteen and that college was still two years down the road. Two years might as well be two minutes as far as time was concerned.

He turned over once more and tried to sleep. The clock said ten-thirty. Outside, the night was cool and still and silent, and he heard his brother's deep regular sleep-breathing in the bed next to his. He wished it would start raining and a clap of thunder would wake up his brother and his brother would see how miserable he was and ask him what was wrong. He knew he would start crying then, but he didn't care. He would tell him that he didn't want him to leave. He would tell him not to take all his clothes out of the closet and put them in a suitcase because he knew that if he did he would never put the clothes back.

His heart was sick with sorrow and nostalgia and grief and the knowledge that even this moment was doomed to pass. He wanted to put his arms around his brother and brace him against time. He wanted to put his arms around him and tell him that he loved him more than anything else in the world, even though it would not make sense in the morning, even though the light would come no matter what he said, no matter how tightly he held him. And the light would find them moving parallel with time, helplessly, stride for stride, no matter what. And soon he himself would be going to college—heartsick, with sideburns and hair under his arms . . . and his father, now mighty, would fall; and his mother, now lovely, would wither.

"Skip?" he said to the darkness. "Skip?"

His brother sniffed and turned over in his sleep.

"Skip?" he said louder.

His brother started, raised his head, and looked around the room.

"What?" he whispered. "What, Will?"

life and times

At this time I am one of the most popular boys in the eighth grade. A year before I was the most popular boy, but times and tastes have changed, and there are now new faces to follow and new places to be led. I have felt the stage turning for six or seven months, but rather than chase the shifting spotlight, I intend to pass into the shadows as proudly and inconspicuously as possible. Still, like an aging politician whose reputation has outlived his actual power, I remain someone to know, someone to be seen with, and certainly someone to watch get beaten up:

the fight

It began with a basketball game. Mike Dichter and I went up for the same rebound, and I accidentally stuck my elbow in his chest. Then Mike stuck his elbow in my chest, pointed a finger at me, and told me to watch out. In those days I had a reputation for toughness to maintain, so I told him that *he* better watch out, and on the next rebound neither of us watched out and both of us got elbows in the chest. Then we started shoving each other under the basket and pointing fingers and making threatening faces, which was fine with me because looking threatening was one of the things I did best.

Before things could get out of hand, however, gym ended, and Mike and I glared at each other and went back to our respective homerooms.

Things probably would have taken a peaceful turn if I hadn't walked home with Kevin Cox after school and told him that the next time Mike and I played basketball I was really going to throw some elbows, and if he, Mike, didn't like it, I would fight him anytime, anywhere. I don't know why I said this. Perhaps I was thinking of the Mike I had known a year before. Perhaps I was thinking of the thin, gullible, good-natured Mike who had since grown four inches, gained fifteen pounds, and become as humorless and menacing as a drill sergeant.

Kevin looked at me doubtfully.

"Do you really think you can take him?" he asked me.

Since Kevin had always been one of my most loyal and servile followers, I was astonished by his doubt in my physical prowess.

"I know I can take him," I said.

"He's three inches taller than you," Kevin said.

"So?"

"He's really strong."

"I'm really strong."

Kevin shrugged. "Okay," he said, "but I think Mike could take you."

Now it was my turn to shrug. It was also my turn to lay a condescending hand upon Kevin's shoulder and leave him to ponder his absurd and traitorous notions.

The next day in school everything proceeded as usual. I listened to the teachers, took notes, fell asleep, made a few uncalled-for remarks, and gazed at Denise Young's legs.

During lunch I was sitting with a tableful of friends, talking and listening in my usual superior way, when I heard Mike Dichter say, "Hey, buddy!" Somehow I knew that he meant me. Somehow I also knew that all kinds of jigs were up and that something momentous was going to happen. I turned to look at him.

"I hear you want to fight me," he said.

"That's right," I said.

"I'll meet you after school."

"I'll be there," I said. Then he walked away, and I discovered two interesting things about myself. The first was that the idea of fighting terrified me, and the second was that in moments of extreme fear my body produced ice-cold sweat.

Someone said something to me, and I smiled and nodded. Someone said something else to me, and I smiled and nodded at that too. Perhaps they were giving me advice. Perhaps they were telling me to stay low and lead with my left. I stood up, without really knowing I was standing up, and walked from the cafeteria to the playground. I had never felt so lonely or so frightened in my life. Somehow I had taken a wrong turn and wound up in the wrong day, in the wrong body, with the wrong future. Somehow, in three hours, I was going to be in a real fight with real fists, and there was no way out of it.

My biggest problem, I knew, was that I didn't hate Mike or even dislike him. I had no animal rage to ball my hands into fists and thrust them into action—no deep-seated envy or resentment to impel me toward him with the object of destruction. All I had was fear and pride, which is a pretty poor combination as far as fighting is concerned, because all pride could do was guarantee that I show up for the fight, and all fear could do was guarantee that I lose it.

The rest of the day passed in a haze of anticipation and dread. I sat through my classes, a smiling silent shell of my former self, and tried to look as casual and confident as possible. Now and then I would look up at the clock and realize that the fight was only one hour and forty-nine minutes away—one hour and forty minutes . . . I tried to tell myself that it might only be a one- or two-punch fight, that maybe Mike would throw a punch and I would throw a punch and we would both smile, throw our arms around each other, and become friends for life. But I knew that it would not be a one- or two-punch fight. No. It would be a fight to some extreme and horrifying limit—a fight to unconsciousness or hospitalization or reconstructive surgery.

During my walks from class to class I discovered that most of the eighth grade had taken sides and that my side consisted of me, a foreign exchange student named Hans, and two girls whose hearts I had not yet broken. The rest of my peers were massed behind Mike, eager to see me put in my place once and for all.

The last class of the day was shop. We were all told by our teacher, Mr. Bledsoe, to work on our special projects. My special project was a skateboard, so I began sanding its nose and trying with all my might not to think about the fight. It is said that there is nothing like working with wood to take one's mind off a problem, but it could also be said that there is nothing like a problem to take one's mind off working with wood. No matter how intensely I sanded the nose of my skateboard, the fight was always with me, and the air around me seemed as thin as Alpine or Himalayan air.

I tried to tell myself that in three hours it would all be over, that I would be in my own house, in my own room, and the fight would be a memory. But three hours would not be enough if I lost the fight. A month would not be enough to heal my humiliation. What would be enough? I asked myself. Six months? No. A year? Yes. A year would be enough. In a year I would be able to look back on this day and smile, or perhaps laugh. In a year the fight would be a distant memory, and I would be a different person with different friends and new reasons to feel confident and proud.

So I closed my eyes and asked God to please make it a year later—to please take me out of this year and place me in the next. With my eyes closed I almost believed that time was racing past me, that eggs were being laid, chicks were being hatched, growing plump, laying their own eggs, and dying.

Unfortunately, when I opened my eyes, I knew that I was still thirteen, still in shop class, and that the fight was waiting to be fought. I thanked God anyway, guessing I had prayed the wrong prayer, looked at the clock, and saw that I had ten minutes left. I did not even try to sand my skateboard those last ten minutes. Instead I drifted into a pleasant state of suspended animation where there was no joy, no fear, no pride, no regret. During this time my pulse rate and respiration dropped, the blood in my veins slowed to a crawl, and I believe I stopped aging.

And then the bell rang, and my time was up.

We were to meet in front of the school. When I got there, I saw a crowd of fifty or sixty people awaiting my arrival. Under different circumstances I would have been pleased by the turnout, but the hopelessness of my position offset whatever theatrical lift I might have felt. I did, however, smile. I was, after all, the other half of the act and was not about to look somber or scared or penitent for anyone.

I saw Mike Dichter standing fifteen or twenty feet away, looking as menacing as ever. He fixed his eyes on me for a moment, then kissed his girlfriend, Linda Lieban. I had foolishly broken up with Linda ten months before. Now, as Mike was kissing her, she looked at me as though she would soon have her revenge.

And then, before I knew it, someone said, "Let's go," and everyone started walking toward the park two blocks away. Strangely, I felt not like a boy on his way to a fight but like a king on his way to the gallows. These were not my classmates before me but peasants in revolt. My wife had already been beheaded, my children sold for horses, my servants set free.

I tried to put everything in perspective, to assure myself that it was only a fight and that losing was no disgrace. And maybe I wouldn't lose. Maybe I was one of those people who did not know his own strength until he was confronted. Maybe when I was facing Mike, some inherited ancient instinct would propel me toward his throat and give me the strength of ten men. My father was certainly a powerful man. My father, at certain times, was one of the most powerful and frightening men I knew. Up to that moment, all I thought I had inherited from him was his pride and his nose, but maybe once I was standing face-to-face with Mike Dichter I would discover that I had inherited his blind rage and lion heart as well.

When we got to the park, a short discussion about the rules of the fight took place. First it was decided that kicking and biting should not be allowed, then that kicking should be allowed, but not scratching. During this time I was standing by a stone water fountain, breathing slowly and wondering when the blood of my father and his father and his father's father was going to show itself. I still couldn't summon enough rage or fury or indignation to make me want to fight Mike or anyone else. All I could do was hope that I was subconsciously feeling those things and was merely biding my time.

"A fight's a fight," I heard someone say. "No bullshit rules."

This motion was contemplated, then carried: Everything allowed. No bullshit rules.

"Should we take our shirts off?" I asked, hoping to postpone things a little longer.

"Whatever," someone said.

And with that all the decisions were made, and there was nothing for Mike and me to do but face each other and fight. Tim Hamilton, our referee, walked us to a clearing and told us to shake hands and fight whenever we were ready. For a moment Mike and I just looked at each other. Then Mike crouched a little, I do not know why, and began to circle me. I knew I should move in and attack immediately, but I was rooted where I stood.

"Fight!" someone said. And now Mike began to advance and kick karate style. The kicks not only served to display his formidable kicking skills but were also a superior defensive and offensive weapon. In order to get to Mike, I would have to find some way to get around his kicks, and in order to do that, I would have to be someone who knew how to fight. My only choice, therefore, was to look unworried and back up, which is what I did. Mike, however, was advancing steadily, which meant that I could either continue backing up until I reached the bus stop on Santa Monica Boulevard or stand my ground and see what happened. Pride demanded that I choose the latter, just in time for Mike to kick me on the thigh. I turned sideways to present a thinner target, bent my knees a little, and took a hard kick to the ribs.

And then things began to happen very quickly. In an instant Mike was on me, and my legs buckled, and we were wrestling on the ground. In an effort to prove that I could fight as dirty as anyone, I gingerly grabbed his groin and discovered that I had neither the will nor the strength to squeeze.

"So that's how you want to play?" Mike said, grabbing *my* groin a good deal less gingerly and wrestling me onto my back. Somehow I was able to get out from under him, and a great deal of grappling, kicking, scratching, and punching ensued while the crowd yelled for either Mike or me to do something that I could not quite make out. Then I saw blood on my shirt and wondered who was bleeding. Before I could find out, Mike was on top of me and my arms were pinned under his knees and he was hitting me very hard in the face. Curiously, I hardly felt the punches. All I felt was the dull impact of the blows, and all I heard were the shrieks and hollers of the crowd, along with the *thump, thump, thump* of fist hitting cheek, ear, chin, forehead, and occasionally mouth. For some reason I was very relaxed. Perhaps because I sensed that I was only getting what I deserved. After all, I had feasted on my own glory and egotism for three years. The check was bound to come.

"Kill him!" I heard Linda Lieban cry. "Kill him!" So Mike reached back and hit me on the side of the head with the hardest punch he had thrown yet.

"Give?" he said.

I shook my head.

"Okay," he said, reaching back to kill me again. He repeated this eight or nine times, and after each punch he said, "Give?" and I said, "No," or shook my head, and he reached back again.

And then, for an instant, I had had enough. For one brief moment the blood of my father and his father and his father's father welled up within me, and I put my hands under Mike's knees, lifted him in the air, held him there, and threw him off me. The crowd gasped, and for a moment Mike looked surprised, even scared.

I stood up to my full height, and the full height of my pride and dignity, but I did not know what to do next. I was no more willing to fight now than I had been before; and the moment passed, and my fury ebbed, and before I knew it, Mike was on top of me picking up where he had left off.

Soon I could not distinguish one punch from another, and my ears burned, and the noises around me seemed to be coming from the other end of a hollow tube. I saw glimpses of faces, but I did not see friends or former friends—all I saw was a crowd, and all I heard was a crowd's noise. I knew it was all over—the love notes, the phone calls, the envy and adulation. Each punch robbed me of another friend, another heart, another follower. From here on out it would just be me, and my TV, and my memories of glory.

And then, one by one, or two by two, the lights went out in my mind, and Mike's legs were around my stomach and I couldn't breathe.

"Give?" he said.

I shook my head.

He squeezed harder. "Give?"

Why not? the last light in my mind said. *All I'm giving him is the fight.* So I gave: I gave him the fight, the love notes, the phone calls, the envy, the adulation, and the arrogant hull of who I had been.

For a moment I felt very light, almost weightless.

o.p.v.

I was working with my brother on my father's vineyard in Fresno and had not gone to the bathroom in six
days. The first day I didn't mind a bit. The second day
I minded a little more and began eating prunes. The
third day I ate cherries, apples, plums, apricots, and
prunes. The fourth day I drank a half gallon of prune
juice and two tablespoons of milk of magnesia. The
fifth day I ate two peanut butter sandwiches, half
of a Sara Lee coffeecake, and twelve doughnuts. On
the morning of the sixth day, I was sluggish, moody,
bloated, and anxious. I had heard about old elephants
walking to nearby caves in order to die with dignity,
and now all I wanted to do was find one of those caves
and die with the elephants. My brother noticed that I
didn't look right and asked me what was wrong.

"I can't go to the bathroom," I said.

"For how long?"

"Six days."

"Have you tried fruit?"

I nodded.

"Prune juice?"

"Everything."

"Milk of magnesia?"

"Everything!"

"Maybe we should call Pop."

For a moment a feeling of relief swept over me, and for the first time in four days I smiled. I smiled because I knew that Pop, aside from being our father, was also a light at the end of a tunnel, a silver lining, and the dawn after a black night. In no time, I knew, my problem would be solved, and I could go back to battling my real problems, which at that time were selfishness, inertia, and a tendency to daydream.

So my brother called Pop, told him my problem, and wrote his advice on a piece of paper. His advice was O.P.V.

"What's O.P.V.?" I asked.

"It's a laxative. He says to take a teaspoon of it and you'll be fine."

I was about to ask why I had never heard of O.P.V. if it was so good, but held my tongue. If I hadn't heard of O.P.V., it was only because it was so special that only a few extraordinary men like my father knew of its existence.

So my brother and I got in the car and drove to the nearest drugstore in search of O.P.V. Three drugstores later we found a dusty box of it on a bottom shelf beside several obscure and similarly dusty brands of toothpaste. All the box said was O.P.V. There was no mention of the word *laxative*, no crass claims of superiority, no slogan. Just O.P.V. and the illustration of a lovely girl in a meadow swinging on a swing with an expression of either relief or ecstasy. Obviously she had once been constipated, but now, with the help of this product, she was free to smile and return to the delightful, carefree life she had certainly been born to. I looked for warnings or cautions on the back of the box and, except for the usual one about frequent or prolonged use of laxatives leading to a dependency upon laxatives, found none. All I saw was a list of herbs, and herbs, I knew, were nature's bounty—healthful, calming, and restorative.

When we went up to the pharmacist to pay, he looked at the box thoughtfully and frowned.

"You sure you boys want this?" he said.

"We're sure," I said, wondering why he, a pharmacist, was not more enthusiastic about this finest of all laxatives.

"Okay," he said in a way that sounded like "It's your funeral" without actually saying it.

During the ride back to the vineyard, I held the box of O.P.V. as if it were a block of gold. I read and reread the list of herbs, fell a little in love with the girl on the swing, and generally felt as though the world were about to become my oyster again.

As soon as we got back to the vineyard, I opened the box and smelled the healthful and restorative aroma of herbs. The herbs were green and looked like tea or shredded dichondra, which, as far as I knew, was exactly the way they were supposed to look. Satisfied, I found a teaspoon, scooped out a mound of O.P.V., and washed it down with water.

"Did Pop say how long it takes to work?"

"I guess about five or six hours," my brother said, which turned out to be an excellent guess because five hours later, while my brother was making homemade ice cream with Inez, the ranch foreman, and his family, I began to feel clammy. This, I knew, was an excellent sign because it meant that the herbs were hard at work clearing a healthful and restorative path through my system. Then my stomach began to cramp a little. At first the cramp surprised me: I had expected something far more pleasant and springlike, but I assured myself that this was only nature's way of righting a six-day wrong and that relief was only minutes away.

The next cramp lasted five seconds and caused me to break out in a light sweat. The cramp after that lasted eight seconds and drained the color from my face. I went into the bathroom, assuming that all I had to do was sit down, but nothing happened—nothing was even close to happening, and the cramping was getting worse. I was still holding fast to the notion that all I had taken were herbs, and that herbs were a natural part of nature, but I couldn't help worrying. Although I had never looked up *paroxysm* in the dictionary, I had heard of the word and knew that I was suffering a paroxysm of pain, or several paroxysms. I also knew that the pain was getting worse and that I was no closer to relief than I had been before I took the laxative.

The next cramp began as an ordinary cramp, then mushroomed into an atomic cramp that obliterated sense, hope, logic, sanity, and self-control. As the pain mounted, I stuck the sleeve of my shirt in my mouth, and when it reached its zenith, I bit a hole in my shirt and pulled the towel rack out of the wall.

Around this time I began to suspect that my father had made a mistake. This suspicion was almost as painful to me as the cramps themselves since, as far as I knew, my father had never given me a wrong piece of advice in his life. I tried to think of some way that he wasn't wrong, but when the next cramp came, I *knew* he was wrong and began thanking him in a loud sarcastic manner.

The next cramp lasted fifteen seconds. In the middle of it I pulled the toilet paper holder out of the wall, leaped to my feet, hurled myself onto the bed, clutched my stomach and made noises I had never made in my life. And then came another cramp. And another. And another. I tried panting to ease the pain; I tried breathing slowly and assuming the fetal position; but nothing worked.

In my short life I had zipped the tip of myself in my zipper, sat on a bumblebee, and accidentally shut a car door on my fingers, but I had never known pain like this. This was pain that could not be overcome with courage, dignity, or discipline; this was pain brought to a science, and I am sure that if I had had a military or governmental secret to divulge, I would have divulged it immediately.

Then I got angry. The pain, I knew, was trying to humble me, and I would not be humbled. I would clench my teeth, dive into the pain like a warrior, and show it who was boss. So when the next cramp came, I dove into the pain with fists figuratively flying. This, however, only made the pain worse, so I tried to dive under the pain as if it were a wave in the ocean. Unfortunately, the pain was bottomless. The only thing below the pain was unconsciousness or death, and I didn't want to dive that deep. So I went the other way and tried to elevate my thoughts to a higher plane—to God and serenity and peace, but the pain dragged me down again, and there was nothing for me to do but pound the bed and try to find peace that way.

When the next cramp came, I decided to go with it—to become a tree that bends but does not break. This felt more natural than anything I had tried yet, so I continued to bend and bend and let the pain blow past me. Then, thinking that this was too much like being humble, I straightened up, gritted my teeth, and leaped into the pain for one last fight. A few seconds into the fight, I realized I had made a mistake and tried to become a tree again, but it was too late, and I was forced to curl up and begin moaning. Maybe I was supposed to make a vow—promise God that I would not do so-and-so forever and ever if He would just make the pain go away. The problem was that I didn't have any really bad habits, and I didn't want to be bound to some promise I had made when I wasn't in my right mind. But I had to do something, so I called out God's name just to let Him know that I knew He was there and that I believed in Him. Then I ran to the bathroom.

An hour later I stuck the towel rack and the toilet paper holder back in the wall, rolled up my shirtsleeve so that the hole didn't show, and fell back onto my bed. How, I wondered, had such a laxative company stayed in business so long, and why did my father take it, and why had he recommended it to me? Of course, it had worked, finally, but the pain, the pain was . . . And then a funny thing happened: I couldn't quite remember what the pain was. I told myself that it had been awful and agonizing and unbearable, but these were only words now that the actual pain was gone, and I wondered if perhaps I had overreacted a little. I had had cramps, of course, and cramps were terribly painful, but had they really been *that* painful? And what were cramps next to this wonderful sense of relief and well-being? Of course, I would never take O.P.V. again—*ever*—and I certainly wouldn't recommend it to my son, when I had a son.

Unless, of course, I *really* needed it—or *he* really needed it.

a short life

The problem was death. Ever since I had learned that it existed and could happen to anyone at any time, I had been on the lookout. Death didn't care that I was almost fourteen and on my way to becoming a world-famous writer. Death didn't care that I was developing a cleft in my chin and a firmer jawline and would consequently be attracting girls and women left and right. Death didn't care that I would soon be shaving and probably revolutionize American fiction before I was twenty-one. Death simply came, boldly or secretly, in the form of a germ or a falling refrigerator, and that was that.

For this reason, I was always on the lookout for symptoms. A sudden loss of eyelashes, a persistent rash, a sore knee—any one of these things could be the first sign of something, and I was determined not to be caught unawares. I did not want to be one of those people who ignore urgent symptoms all their life, only to discover that they have been quietly decomposing for months. I did not want some doctor to tell me, "I wish you had seen me a month ago," or, "It seems to have gotten out of hand." Some might have called me a hypochondriac, but I didn't care. As long as life was fleeting and man was mortal, I was going to expect the worst.

Therefore, when I felt the lump on my head, I knew it was a tumor. I knew it was a tumor because I had seen a television drama two nights before about a boy just like me who had a lump on his head. In one hour I watched this boy go from a strapping, clear-eyed, clean-cut, straight-A student to a prone, pasty-faced shadow of his former self. Having read the synopsis of the program in *TV Guide*, I knew the boy's fate even as he was throwing perfect passes to his receivers and making surprise runs for touchdowns. I knew why he had a slight headache after the game, and why he felt dizzy after he kissed his girlfriend, and why he fainted in the shower, but I didn't expect things to deteriorate so sadly or so traumatically. The drama ended with the boy bravely telling his girlfriend that he would still escort her to the senior prom, but, of course, he probably wouldn't, and I knew it and he knew it and his girlfriend knew it too. The camera froze on his pale face, then the screen went to black.

And now *I* had the tumor and would never marry, never see Spain, never win the Nobel Prize. I made a quick check of my diminishing motor skills by throwing a cigarette into the air and trying to catch the filter end in my teeth, and, sure enough, the cigarette bounced off my nose and landed on the bathroom floor.

Soon, I knew, I would not be able to wink or smile or make a fist. I felt the lump again and tried to remember if something had fallen on my head in the last two days, but, of course, nothing had. The lump was a tumor, and my fate was sealed.

Well, I wasn't going to be a coward about it. I wasn't going to deteriorate into a puddle of tears and self-pity. I was going out with my head held high. I was going to stand for something in sickness the way other men stood for something in health. Anyway, it would be the world's loss, not mine. I would still be me somewhere, but where would the world be? Where would the future of American fiction be?

And maybe I was wrong. Maybe it was just a bump or a benign lump, and all was well. I would ignore it. I would do my homework and live my life and stop letting my imagination get the better of me. For once in my life I was going to stop acting like a mouse, an old woman, and a malingerer and take hold of the reins of my imagination.

Full of resolve, I looked at myself in the mirror, frowned, clenched my teeth, and willed myself to forget about the tumor. Then I stormed out of the bathroom, sat down at my desk, ripped open my history book, and began doing my homework. *You are a rock*, I told myself. *Your mind is a rock.* So I read and read, my mind like a rock, but I wasn't absorbing anything—the words in the history book were simply washing over my mind. So I softened my mind a little, just enough to absorb words, and started to read again. Just as I was beginning to concentrate, I absently put my hand on the side of my head and felt the lump. Helplessly, I began probing the lump, and my mind went completely soft again. *I'm dying*, I thought.

I went into the bathroom and looked at myself in the mirror. The skin on my face seemed tighter than usual, and my eyes looked a little cloudy. I tried once again to toss a cigarette in the air and catch it in my mouth, but again it hit my nose and fell on the floor. *All right, then, I'm dying*, I thought. *No first love, no Paris, no Rome, no novels, no wife, no children, no house in Jamaica, no fame, no adventure.* I shrugged my shoulders resignedly, smiled at my reflection in the mirror, panicked, walked quickly to my mother's room, and asked her to feel the lump.

"What do you think?" I asked.

"About what?"

"The lump. Don't you feel it?"

"That's your head, William."

"The lump is my head?"

"Of course."

"You're sure it's not a tumor?"

"Of course not."

"Of course you're *not* sure it's not a tumor, or of course you're *sure* it's not a tumor?"

"Of course it's not a tumor. You have a bumpy head."

"That's all?"

"That's all."

"Thank you," I said. And I stood up and left her room — wondering why the first finger of my right hand felt a little numb.

the bird hunter

As far as I knew, no one in my family had ever killed a bird in his or her life. My father had killed a jackrabbit once, on his vineyard, but that was because the jackrabbit was either digging holes or eating the grapes or attacking the smaller animals who were somehow beneficial to the soil or the vines or the grapes themselves.

Nevertheless, one morning when I was twelve years old, I knew I had to kill a bird. Actually, it wasn't so much the killing end that I wanted to be on as much as the shooting end. I wanted to forget for a moment that I was only twelve years old with a B-minus average, a retainer, and a knack for being sent to the vice-principal's office. I wanted to whip out my cousin's CO_2 cartridge–powered BB gun, crouch like a secret agent, swivel, fire, and change the world slightly. Anyway, I knew that twelve-year-olds had been shooting birds for years and that the birds saw nothing, heard nothing, and felt nothing. One minute they were flying or chirping, and the next they weren't.

So one morning I tucked the BB gun in my pants and set out with my friends Kevin and Tim for Kevin's grandmother's house. Ostensibly, we were going there to play tennis, so I brought my tennis racket along just in case Kevin's grandmother got suspicious. This turned out to be an unnecessary precaution since Kevin's grandmother was very old and stayed in the living room with the door closed most of the time. Her backyard, however, was a sportsman's paradise: there were birds everywhere. Birds flying from tree to tree, birds walking on the grass, birds sitting on hedges, and birds cleaning themselves in the birdbath. There was also a solitary bird perched on a telephone wire, and this bird, I decided, would be my first target.

After firing a few practice shots into the ivy, I tucked the gun back into my pants, turned my back on the bird, whipped out the gun, swiveled, crouched, and fired. The bird did not move. Nor did the telephone wire. I had heard stories about faulty guns that shot high or low or left or right, so I aimed above the bird's head and fired. Nothing. I aimed below the bird's feet and fired. Nothing. I aimed left and fired, and right and fired. The bird chirped and flew away. At that same instant I saw a bird on a hedge and fired twice—then, hearing a sound that might have been a bird, I swiveled and fired into the trees.

"You're not concentrating," Tim said.

"I'm concentrating," I said. "I think I have a faulty gun." I proved this by shooting at the telephone pole and missing.

Then I remembered that real hunters did not shoot wildly at their prey. They stalked, they lurked. So I began stalking the backyard—not in a way that would embarrass me in front of my friends, but casually, subtly. I also remembered that hunters walked on light feet, so I began walking lightly, though, again, not in a way that would seem too unlike my usual way of walking.

I ambled soundlessly over to the birdbath, shot a glance at the roof of the house, saw a bird, fired three times, and missed. Then I lost my temper and began shooting at trees, hedges, and dichondra.

Tim and Kevin started laughing.

"Give it up," Kevin said.

I was too angry to speak, so I said nothing. It was going to be one more lost game of Monopoly, one more roll of Scotch tape on my head, one more drooling kiss, one more failure ordained by a universe that had smugly decreed that I would forever be its plaything, its puppet, its fool. With this in mind, my desire to kill a bird began to border on an obsession. I had come to kill a bird, and I was going to kill a bird.

The problem was that all the birds were gone. I glanced behind the patio chairs, circled the birdbath, and looked up at the telephone wires. Then I stopped and listened for the sound of chirping. I heard nothing. So I tucked my gun in my pants, covered it with my shirt, sat down by the side of the tennis court and, with a casual and disinterested expression, watched Tim and Kevin play tennis. I did this in order to trick the birds into thinking I had changed my mind about everything and that it was safe for them to return.

A few minutes later I heard a cautious chirp or tweet, but I did not stir. I did not even move my head. Soon the chirps became more bold and numerous, and I knew that the birds were back. While pretending to yawn, I secretly surveyed the entire backyard. There was not a bird in sight. They were back in the trees, but they were watching—making sure. So I stopped yawning and watched Kevin win the third and final set, six to four.

"We gotta go," he said.

"Not yet," I said.

"We have to. I told my mom I'd be back at three."

I was about to beg him for five more minutes, when I saw it. A BIRD. It was standing just behind the baseline at the opposite end of the court.

"Shhh," I said, pulling the gun out of my pants and silently crossing the tennis court. I moved in almost slow motion, my eyes never leaving my prey. When I was standing opposite it, I froze, certain that if I advanced another step, the bird would fly for cover.

The bird was fifteen feet away now, which meant that I would have to aim down and at an angle—an impossible shot. What I needed was a level shot. But how? In answer to that question, I lay down on my belly so that the bird was in my direct line of fire. Then I raised the gun an inch off the ground, took a deep breath, held the breath, and fired. *Phhht!* Instantly, the bird fell over on its side.

"I hit it!" I cried. "I hit it!"

I looked over at my friends for some sign of awe or approbation, then ran over to the bird. Because nothing I had ever seen on TV had ever taken more than one shot to kill, I knew that the bird would be in perfect dead repose—its breast still, its eyes closed. Only, when I got to the bird, I saw that it wasn't dead—in fact, its eyes were open and its chest was heaving.

At first all I could do was look on in horror. I had no idea that this was what hunting meant and was completely unprepared to face the living consequences of my actions.

Then the bird began flapping its wings, and something sickening stirred in my blood. Frantically, I shot it again, this time in the chest, and still its eyes did not close and its wings did not stop flapping. And suddenly I realized that my gun might be useless, that there might be no way of putting this bird out of its misery. I thought of stepping on its head, but I couldn't do it, so I shot it again, three, four, five times, and the BBs made little red dots on its chest and its neck, but it still wouldn't die. It was simply filling up with BBs, each of which had the power to inflict agony, and none of which had the power to kill it. Then I began to think that I would never kill it, that all the BBs in the world weren't enough to kill it; and suddenly there was no tennis court, no trees, no sky, no sun, no world—there was just me firing BBs into the bird, and the bird's body absorbing the BBs and waiting for death. And every unnecessary instant of that bird's agony felt like an eternity to me, for I was the bird now as much as myself, and its misery was mine, and I felt each BB enter my heart or my throat or my stomach or my chest. In desperation, I put the mouth of the gun to the bird's head and fired four times—and it was over.

Kevin, Tim, and I gathered up the tennis balls, put them in cans, and started past the open gate to the sidewalk. I tried to shrug off the murder and not let my friends see how I really felt. I'd never really trusted them, for the same reason that bird couldn't trust me; and I walked home alone that day, feeling as ghastly as the first man after he'd taken a bite of the wrong fruit in the Garden of Eden.

skip leaving for college

All the packing. The emptying of closets, the folding of shirts, the buying of blankets, the cleaning out of the desk that meant my brother, my roommate, my friend and companion was going away to college. No more drives in the red convertible, no more eight p.m. runs for pizza, no more "good night, Skip," "good night, Will," no more comforting sound of sleep-breathing in the bed next to mine.

He told me that he would come home for Thanksgiving and Christmas and every summer vacation. He told me that it would be like he had never left, but I knew that nothing would ever be the same again; I knew that I would never be happy, or if I was, it would be a hollow, qualified kind of happiness.

He was leaving on a Sunday, which had always been a bad day anyway—a day of endings, of barbecues and false cheer and sad dusky evenings. As the day of his departure approached, we swam, golfed, bowled, and played football and baseball like never before.

And then came the second-to-last golf game, the last golf game, the last pizza, the last long drive, the last catch of the football, the last swing of the bat.

"Good night, Skip."

"Good night, Will."

The next day began slowly, the moments passing like black Cadillacs on their way to a gravesite. We said the same things we usually said to each other in the morning, but there was a sentence of change hanging over the day that made everything we said sound tragic and gloomy. I kept hoping that Skip would change his mind at the last minute, or get the flu, or sprain his ankle. Or perhaps someone would tell him that he couldn't go; or he would not want to go.

And then the moments began to gather speed, began narrowing to a destiny, and before I knew it, breakfast was over, and then he had showered and then he was dressed and then he was carrying his suitcases to his car and hugging Pop and hugging Mom and hugging Carol and hugging me; and I longed to go backward in time, to relive the last two years, the last month, the last week over and over again for the rest of my life. And every time I reached this moment, I would bounce back through time to the days when I was in Little League and no one had to go anywhere.

life and times

I am a sophomore in high school. Life is smooth —blue skies and swimming pools. When I am not looking in the mirror, I am tanning, and when I am not tanning, I am writing short stories or playing touch football or falling in love or having delightful dreams about some wonderful girl who I am sure I will meet soon.

I know that I will revolutionize American fiction before I am twenty. I know that every word I write should be chiseled in stone or bronzed or recited by Laurence Olivier.

On days when I have pimples, I keep my head down and walk quickly. I listen to Gordon Lightfoot love songs and reread romantic passages from The Great Gatsby *and* The Sun Also Rises.

I have perfected looking mysterious, knowing, and preoccupied by philosophical thoughts. I gaze into space whenever possible and stride down the school halls looking like the poster boy for Self-Possession. Talking, I realize, can only spoil my image, so I say as little as possible in school. My job is to rise above things, and stay there. The only problem is I'm flunking geometry:

91

my tutor

No one had ever tried harder to understand geometry than I had, but from the first day it was hopeless. I sat at my desk in the back row looking and listening with all my might while our teacher, Mr. Carravacci, explained that AXB was somehow equal to XBM if the value of B was three and X was a variable. Then he proceeded to draw letters and brackets on the blackboard for twenty minutes, saying things like "value" and "proofs" and "bisect" and "congruent." He also said "therefore" a great deal, perhaps five or six times more than most people say it in their entire lives; and by the end of the class, I knew that if geometry was the study of logic and numbers, and if the understanding of logic and numbers was necessary to pass geometry, then I was going to spend a great deal of my life in Mr. Carravacci's class.

I do not remember if my geometry tutor was recommended by the school, or a friend of my mother, or Mr. Carravacci himself, but one way or another the doorbell rang one Tuesday afternoon and I opened the door. I had expected to see a serious, middle-aged, bespectacled mathematician with graying temples, a high forehead, and a competent, businesslike air. What I saw was a frail-looking seventy-five-year-old woman with feathery white hair, milky blue eyes, and a polite, almost deferential expression. She asked me in a voice that was only a year or perhaps six months from quavering if I was Billy, and I said that I was Will, and she said that her name was Mrs. March. I invited her into the house, and as she passed by me, I smelled the scent of her perfume and something else that made the perfume smell like an empty wood closet.

When we got to my room, we sat down at my desk and I showed her my homework.

"I'm having trouble with the isosceles triangle proof," I said.

"I see," Mrs. March said. She said it as if we were two guests at a party making polite conversation, instead of a student and his tutor trying to keep the student from flunking, so I added, "Maybe you can help me."

After a moment or two of silence, Mrs. March said, "With . . . ?"

"The isosceles triangle proof," I said. I pointed at my homework. "Here."

"Oh, yes, yes, of course," Mrs. March said.

She looked over the paper for fifteen or twenty seconds, then looked at me.

"And what don't you understand, Alan?"

"Well," I said, "they want me to prove that angle ABC is equal to ACB, and I can't do it."

"All right," Mrs. March said. Then she studied the triangle again and looked at me.

"I understand the first part," I said. "I know that AB equals AC."

"Then let's write that down," Mrs. March said with a voice that forty years ago must have sounded brisk and efficient. She opened her notebook, and in a small, slightly tremulous hand wrote *AB equals AC*. "Now," she said, "we know that AB equals AB."

"AC," I said.

"AC," Mrs. March said. "Have you a glass of water, Alan?"

"Of course," I said. I got her a glass of water, which she drank.

"Thank you," she said. And then she was silent and stayed silent.

"Mrs. March?"

"Yes, Alan."

"AB equals AC."

"Oh, yes. Well, let's see . . ." And she looked at the triangle for a while, then at the letters she had written, and I realized that she might be eighty rather than seventy-five and that her grasp of geometry was not as sure as it had once been.

"I know we're supposed to bisect the triangle," I said.

"Oh, I'm sorry," Mrs. March said. "You're right. I

94

don't know what's wrong with me today. Of course. Bisect the triangle."

So we bisected the triangle into ABD and ACD.

"Now we have two congruent triangles," Mrs. March said. "ABD and ACD. What does that tell us?"

I was silent, of course, because I had no idea, and Mrs. March was silent because she had no idea either.

"Maybe we should go to another problem," I said. "We can always come back to this one."

"No, no," Mrs. March said. "Let's always finish what we start. Now, what do we know?"

"We know that ABD equals ACD."

"And what do we know if we know that ABD equals ACD?"

"That we have bisected a triangle."

"Very good," Mrs. March said. "Now we can go on to the next problem."

"But we haven't proved that ABC is equal to ACB," I said.

"Oh, my," Mrs. March said. "Oh, my . . ."

So we both looked at the problem again and lapsed into another long silence.

"May I see your book, Alan?" Mrs. March said.

I handed her my book, which she studied.

"Isn't that funny," she said. "Now I know ABD is equal to ACD, and I know AB is equal to AC, but why . . . ?" She left the sentence unfinished.

"Maybe we should go on to the next problem," I said, and this time she didn't argue. She just looked at me as though I might be able to tell her why she no longer knew now what she had once known so well before.

So we went on to the next problem, and Mrs. March asked me what we knew and what we could assume, and I told her I didn't know, and we lapsed into many silences, and after each silence Mrs. March shook her white head and said she didn't know what was wrong with her today, and I felt a little strange because I knew that forty years ago she had known the solutions to all these problems, and her eyes had been royal blue, and her hand did not shake, and her hair wasn't white, and her voice was clear and strong, and she didn't have to apologize to anyone.

We went on to the next problem, and the next problem after that until it was five-thirty and time for Mrs. March to leave. I escorted her slowly down the stairs, across the hall to the front door, and handed her a twenty-dollar check.

"Oh, no," Mrs. March said. "I couldn't take that."

"Why?"

"No, no, Alan. I wasn't very good today."

"You were very good today, Mrs. March," I said. "Please take it."

So Mrs. March finally took the check because it was a portion of food or rent, or twenty percent of a car payment, or seventy-five percent of a heating bill, and thanked me and walked out the door.

After I closed the door, I stood in the hall for a moment, smiled, and as a sort of epitaph to the last hour and a half, shook my head resignedly. As far as I was concerned, the episode was over and all I had to do was find myself another tutor. I still felt a little strange, but this, I assumed, was because I needed air, so when I got to my room, I opened all the windows and breathed deeply for several minutes—in and out, in and out, right up until the time I started to cry.

emily

As far as my family was concerned, I had gone with my brother to work on our uncle's vineyard in Arvin in order to earn enough money to spend two weeks in Hawaii. But truly, I had gone for the same reason I went anywhere in those days: to find love. In those days a path was only worth following if it led to love, a box was only worth opening if it contained love; and romantic love, when I was sixteen, was a path I could not find—a box within a box within a box. I had not found it in grammar school, and I could not find it in high school, but I knew that it was somewhere and that it was waiting.

The drive to Arvin from our uncle's house in Bakersfield took twenty minutes. While my brother drove, I would sit back in my seat, watch the red sun rise over the green valley, inhale the fragrance of ripe grapes, fertile soil, and healthy vines, and daydream. I had discovered that I was a writer by then, which meant that my daydreaming was valid and perhaps even profitable. Toward the end of our journey, we would pass a small wooden farmhouse that stood a little off the road in the middle of nothing. The farmhouse had a green corrugated iron roof, a stovepipe chimney, a peeling white fence, and a sagging wood-plank porch. At first it was only a curiosity, a decrepit wooden square with a roof, an impossible habitation to one who had been brought up in Beverly Hills. But a few days later I saw a light in the window, and the light animated the farmhouse and made me wonder who lived there. Probably a farmer and his wife, I supposed—a kind, hardworking man of forty-five and a lovely woman of forty. Perhaps they even had a daughter.

The next day, as we drove past the farmhouse, I knew that the daughter was a soft, frail beauty with ivory-white skin, lavender eyes, and blond hair. I could almost see her in her poor white nightgown devotedly serving her parents the breakfast she had made them. I could see her delicate white hands laying fried eggs upon chipped plates and pouring hot coffee into stained cups.

"Thank you, Emily," her father would say. "Would you like to say grace?"

And, of course, Emily would. And her voice would be as soft and modest and true as an angel's, and when she finished, she would raise her eyes and begin to eat.

The next morning as we drove past the farmhouse, I decided that Emily was not only shy and modest and true, but lonely as well. I could see her lying in her bed at night gazing at the moon outside her open window and listening to the deep silence of the valley. I could see her kneeling in the darkness on the sagging wooden floor of her bedroom praying for a man to love.

"Will?" my brother said.

"What?" I snapped.

"Were you sleeping?"

"No. Just thinking about Hawaii."

That night I lay in bed thinking about Emily. I decided that she was a simple girl, pure of heart, who never left the farmhouse except to buy sugar or shoes. I also decided that she loved animals and was afraid of the dark. Someday, I knew, I would knock on her door, and she would open the door and see me and know that I was the man she had been waiting for.

"I'm William," I would say.

"I'm Emily."

"I know."

"How do you know?"

"Because I've known you all my life—the same way you've known me."

And she would blush and lower her eyes and invite me in for breakfast. After breakfast she would invite me to stay for the day, and after that day she would invite me to stay with her forever.

———————

Things went on like this for one week. Every morning, as my brother and I drove to work, I thought only of Emily. I knew she held some secret for me—the secret of the womb or of the ocean depths—and I longed to learn that secret. I longed to sit on the rotted-wood porch with her on a summer evening and hold her close to me and forget about being a writer and famous and sophisticated and well-traveled. I longed to lie beside her at night under her worn blanket beneath the pale light of her lamp and feel her heart beat against mine. Outside her window we would watch the white moon over the vineyards—a moon as pale and mysterious and innocent as Emily.

One morning, as my brother and I approached the farmhouse, I knew that I was ready to become a farmer; ready to embrace the rural life of vines and grapes and soil and summer; ready to learn how to drive a tractor and spread seeds and make lemonade and wear overalls and bid my old life goodbye. All I had to do was find out if Emily existed.

"Stop the car," I said.

"What?"

"Just stop at that farmhouse for a second. I want to see something."

My brother pulled over to the side of the road.

"What are you going to do?" he asked.

"I'm going to knock on that door."

"Why?"

"I'm looking for someone," I said.

I got out, closed the car door, and began walking toward the farmhouse feeling as purposeful and emboldened by destiny as any man had ever felt. Then, when I was only ten or fifteen yards away, I suddenly glimpsed the reality of what I was doing, and I was no longer a prince mounting the palace steps to claim my beloved but a sixteen-year-old boy walking on real dirt toward the front door of a dilapidated farmhouse at five-forty-five in the morning to meet a girl who could not possibly live there. Furthermore, I was going to knock on that door, disrupt the life or lives of whoever lived there, and try to explain who I was and why I had come. For a moment I thought of turning back and telling my brother it had all been a mistake. But it was too late. I had to know if Emily was there. So I kept walking, my hands wet, my heart pounding. When I reached the front door, I hesitated, took a deep breath, and knocked. After several seconds the door opened, and an old man who did not look at all like Emily's father was staring at me.

"Hello," I said, trying to catch my breath. "My name is William."

He waited.

"Uh, do you have a daughter, sir?"

As soon as I asked the question, I knew that he didn't; I knew that all he had was the farmhouse and a tin coffee cup and maybe a bad temper.

"A daughter?"

"Yes, a—a blond, fair-skinned . . . about my age?"

"Who are you?"

"My name is William."

"And you want to know if I have a daughter?"

"Yes, sir. A blond, fair-skinned . . ."

It was hopeless. I knew it was hopeless. It was just a

shack on a vineyard in a valley, but I decided to give it one last try.

"Do you happen to know anyone by the name of Emily?"

"Emily?" He didn't understand.

"Someone about my age?"

"Why do you want to know?"

"She's just someone I met. She told me she lived around here."

"You're looking for a girl?"

"One particular girl, yes sir."

"Well, I'm sorry. She's not here. I live alone."

"I see. Well . . ." He closed the door.

When I got back to the car, my brother said, "What was that all about?"

"Nothing," I said.

"Who were you looking for?"

I didn't want to tell him, but it didn't seem to matter anymore, so I said, "A girl."

"What girl?" he asked.

So I told him all about Emily—about her white nightgown and her ivory-white skin and her blond hair and her lavender eyes. When I finished, I felt a little foolish, but he looked at me as though I was not foolish at all and said, "Maybe she'll be in Hawaii."

carrots

He knew that his father yelled now and then, but usually he yelled for a good reason, and all he had done was hold on to the carrot sticks. He was sure he had held them at dinner before. He had always held on to them. And now the room was dark and he couldn't sleep.

But what had he really done wrong? Obviously, people weren't supposed to hold on to carrot sticks with one hand while they ate with the other, but why hadn't he heard about this before? Why hadn't someone told him? Usually they told you first, then they yelled. He had obviously made an enormous mistake.

"What the hell are you doing?" his father had said. "Take the carrots out of your hand and put them on the plate!"

And suddenly the table was silent, and his brother and sister looked down at their plates.

"He doesn't know, Ross," his mother had said, seemingly surprised herself by the outburst.

"Why doesn't he know? For Christ's sake, it's simple: Put the carrots on the plate, pick up a carrot, eat the carrot, then pick up another carrot. What the hell's wrong with him?"

And it was sad because it wasn't the old anger righting an actual wrong. It was something else that had nothing to do with carrots. And he wanted to look at his father, but he couldn't do it. He couldn't do anything but finish his meal and ask to be excused from the table.

And now it was eight o'clock and he was lying in his bed and he still didn't know what had happened. He knew that from now on he would keep the carrots on the plate. He knew that he would always eat the carrot sticks one at a time. But he was still confused.

And then he heard footsteps on the stairs, and he knew they were his father's footsteps. His father looked into the room. "Are you awake?"

Even in the dark he could feel the sweetness of his father's presence, could hear it in his voice.

"Yes," he said.

His father came into the room, and he could feel the room diminish in size, become a playroom with play furniture and paper walls. His father's presence was so real, so strong that everything around it seemed make-believe.

"You know," his father said, sitting down on his brother's bed, "sometimes when I get angry at you, I'm really angry about other things. Sometimes something will happen in town or at the office, and instead of yelling about that, I yell about the carrots, or the plates, or something else. You understand that, don't you?"

"Yes," he said, though he did not really understand anything except the feeling of his father's presence and the tenderness of his voice.

"And you know that I love you even when I yell at you?"

"Yes."

"Good," his father said, leaning close to him and kissing him on the cheek. "Now go to sleep."

"Good night, Pop," he said, and his voice was small because his heart had swelled right up to his Adam's apple.

"Good night."

And then he was in the dark again, but not alone because his father had been there, would always be there.

karate

After I had been beaten senseless in a fight in the
eighth grade, I lost a good deal of my sense of humor and
took to staying in my room, frowning at imaginary foes in
the bathroom mirror, and dreaming of invincibility. I still
looked like myself, and talked and sounded like myself,
but now I could not walk down the school halls without
wondering if I could take this or that boy in a fight. All
my thoughts centered on fighting: I punched the air in
my room when I returned home from school, I kneed the
air in the groin just before dinner, and I elbowed the air
in the stomach just before bedtime. My new self, I decided, would be calm, confident, and subtly terrifying.
When people met me, they would sense immediately that
I was dangerous, inviolable. At five foot six and a hundred and ten pounds, I knew that I was neither dangerous nor inviolable, so I decided to take karate.

My instructor was a man by the name of Casey
Farouk. Before I met him, I assumed he would be a tall
man with gray eyes and a cruel mouth—a man brim-

ming with the kind of confidence that comes when one can leap five feet in the air and paralyze any foe. But when the doorbell rang for my first lesson and I opened the door, I saw a pale, balding, sickly-looking man with arms almost as thin and unmuscled as my own.

"I am Casey Farouk," he said in the highest voice, male or female, I had ever heard. I could not imagine such a man jumping five feet into the air and paralyzing anyone, so after I led him into the living room, I asked him if he would please demonstrate a flying kick.

Casey smiled, walked to the center of the room, leaped like a cat, kicked, landed, and looked at me.

"Now," he said, "why do you want to take karate?"

I told him about the fight, and how I had been beaten up in front of all my friends and that I never wanted to lose another fight again. I told him that I wanted to become a karate master and move as fast as lightning. While I spoke, my face grew red and my voice rose with a passion that was perhaps a millimeter shy of psychosis.

Casey looked impressed. "Okay," he said.

That day I learned what to do if a man had a gun at my back, a knife at my throat, or a grip on my shirt collar. I also learned how to block a punch and stop someone from choking me. At the end of the lesson, Casey told me that I had great promise, bowed, and took my father's check for thirty-five dollars.

———————

In the next two months my reflexes and sense of self-preservation became as highly developed as a rabbit's or an antelope's. In fact, I was so high-strung that I had trouble sleeping and tended to flinch when someone unexpectedly patted my shoulder or said hello. I learned how to bend at the knees, swivel, punch, advance, retreat, kick, scream, fall, duck, and roll. Every morning before school I stretched, punched the air, and advanced karate-style to my bedroom door; every night I did seventy-five push-ups, seventy-five sit-ups, and disarmed invisible assailants. Sometimes I would go to my sister's room and ask her to attack me with a pencil or grab my collar or try to hold me from behind. Then, with blinding speed, I would either break the pencil or reverse the hold, or break the hold and steal the pencil, and my sister would tell me how proud she was of me, and I would go back to my room and kick and roll and tumble and duck until it was time for bed.

Casey said that I was the best student he had ever had and that at the rate I was progressing I would become a black belt faster than anyone he had ever known, including himself. I knew he was telling the truth because I could disarm him or throw him over my knee almost at will, and whenever we wrestled, it was he who cried in pain. He called me "Killer."

In school I strode up and down the halls with the calm knowledge that I was almost invincible. It did not matter that my ears were still a little purple from the fight, that girls ignored me and boys laughed behind my back. What mattered was that the muscles under my shirt were growing bigger every day and that I was secretly on my way to becoming a lethal human being.

When my brother came home from college, I couldn't wait to demonstrate all the new things I had learned. I couldn't wait because he had always been my physical superior, and I wanted to show him, in a friendly way, that things had changed. And so, as he and his friend Bob Kaloff looked on, I did seventy-five push-ups, ten one-arm push-ups, and lifted myself from a headstand to a handstand. Then I advanced and retreated karate-style across the carpet, blocked kicks, and threw punches.

Then I told my brother to choke me.

"Are you sure, Will?" he said. "I don't want to hurt you."

"You won't hurt me," I said. "Just choke me. You'll see."

So he stood up, put his hands around my throat and began choking me. Then, in one swift and seamless motion, I raised my arms over my head, swiveled left to break his hold, and—and his arms were like girders and he was still choking me. Desperately, I repeated the motion, but his arms held and his hands were still clutching my throat and I couldn't breathe.

"Do you want me to let go?" he asked.

"Yes," I said.

Here my brother smiled. It was a compassionate smile, I suppose, but I interpreted it as a challenge to the last three months of my life.

"All right," I said, my anger and frustration rising, "stand behind me and put your arms around me tight— as tight as you can."

"As tight as I can?"

"Just put your arms around me," I said.

My brother did so, and my arms sort of collapsed inward toward my chest. I tried to bend my knees, but I couldn't move—I couldn't begin to move, and I knew that there would be no maneuvering of my left leg behind his, no leverage, no unbalanced body toppling to the ground; there would be only me caught in the viselike embrace of my brother and time and the limitations of a thirteen-year-old body that would never be strong enough or old enough or agile enough. As the seeds of humiliation began to sprout within me, I summoned every bit of strength I had and tried to break his hold or bend my knees, but it didn't work. And then I knew that all the months of struggle and sweat and push-ups and sit-ups had come to nothing and that I was still my brother's little brother, still the same boy who had been beaten up in the park eleven Mondays before, and every ounce of my rage and frustration welled within me, and my brother said, "Okay, Will?" and I nodded, and he released his arms, and I started to cry. Then, my brother, seeing what had happened, and perhaps why it had happened, held up his hands for me to hit, and I hit them and hit them as hard as I could—left, right, left, right—like a boxer, and still crying—left, right, left, right—until I stopped crying and my brother's hands were red.

five dollars an hour

I was walking down my sixty-first row of the day looking for large treelike weeds. When I found a large weed, I loosened the soil around it with my shovel, tried to lift it out by hand, and if I couldn't, I'd dig it up with the shovel. I had been walking up and down rows of vines since nine o'clock in the morning. It was a hundred and five degrees and I was becoming delirious.

I made up two or three songs and began singing. Then, when the heat sapped my will to sing, I began thinking about movie stars I liked. I thought about Claudia Cardinale for two rows, Senta Berger for three rows, and Jane Fonda for four rows.

Then I pretended that I was a hale and hearty farmer, and I smiled broadly and walked with long hearty strides. This lasted for about half a row. Then I was a seventy-five-year-old weather-beaten peasant who had been working in the sun all his life. My name was José and I had ten children, twenty-five grandchildren, and a sick wife. I tried to love the vines and the grapes and the sun and the soil in the wise and spiritual way José would have, and I did for two rows.

Then I began talking to myself: "Once when I was fourteen," I told Johnny Carson, "I worked on my father's vineyard in Fresno."

"Was it hard?" Johnny asked me.

"It was backbreaking, impossible work," I said.

"Do you think it helped you win the Nobel Prize for literature?"

"I do. Yes. The discipline I learned on that ranch made me a better writer and a better human being."

"You were brought up in Beverly Hills, weren't you?"

"Yes. I was."

"That must have been quite a change."

"Oh, it was a change, all right. But I'm glad I did it. I'm glad I did it. I'm glad I did it. I'm glad I did it. I'm glad I did it." I said this phrase over and over, until the words lost their meaning. Then I said, "Hot day, hot, hot, hot, hot day," twenty or thirty times. Then I sang "The Banana Boat Song."

I hadn't expected this. I hadn't expected to wake up at five o'clock in the morning and work until four o'clock in the afternoon. I hadn't expected to paint fence posts near a swamp and get sixty mosquito bites and walk up and down rows of vines in one-hundred-and-five-degree heat and paint bunkhouses and scrape paint off cement and turn canes and uproot treelike weeds and be leg-, arm-, chest-, neck-, back-, and foot-weary. To make matters worse, my brother had gotten it into his head that we were going to make Pop proud. As he saw it, the only way to make Pop proud was to work harder and longer than was safe or natural. In order to convince me that I could work harder and faster if I wanted to, he put a block of ice on his face and let it melt all the way down until it fit into his mouth. Then he sucked it until it disappeared. "See, Will?" he said. "Anything's possible."

And to top it off, I didn't know how much money I was making. My brother told me that when all the work was over, Pop would ask us what we thought we were worth per hour. Minimum wage was a dollar an hour, and by my calculations I was worth five times that, so I would say, "I'm worth five dollars an hour, Pop." If he looked surprised, I would simply repeat the figure. If he asked me why I was worth five dollars an hour, I would say, "Because I have sixty mosquito bites and have worked harder in hotter weather than anyone has ever worked in their life. Because I painted the bunkhouse, and walked up and down rows of vines until I nearly fainted, and am leg-, arm-, back-, and footweary. I am worth five dollars an hour, Pop, because no one in their right mind would do this kind of work for less than twenty dollars an hour."

Five dollars an hour was the least I could expect for having been tricked into this kind of work. And make no mistake about it, I *had* been tricked. My father had said, "How would you like to work in Fresno for three weeks?" and I had said, "Fine." My father had not said, "How would you like to work nine hours a day in one-hundred-and-five-degree heat trudging up and down endless rows of vines until everything aches and you begin talking to yourself?" If my father had said that, I would have said, "No, thank you," and would now be in Beverly Hills getting a tan and perhaps falling in love with someone.

And so I was going to stand up for myself, look my father in the eye and tell him exactly what I was worth.

The only problem was that my father was a hard man to look in the eye and say "Good morning" to, much less "I believe I am worth five dollars an hour." He was so decisive and forthright himself that he made everyone else's forthrightness seem like a challenge or some new kind of crookery. The last thing I wanted to do, of course, was challenge my father, but I was still going to ask for five dollars an hour. Even if I had to whisper it.

Two weeks later, when all the work was over, my brother and I were sitting with Pop in the ranch office we had converted into our bedroom. I had forgotten just how dynamic and intimidating my father's presence could be, even in repose, and wondered for a moment if four dollars and fifty cents might be a more reasonable sum. *No*, I thought. *I am worth five dollars, and that is what I am going to ask for.*

After a few minutes of pleasant conversation, the question finally came:

"Well, William," my father said, "what do you think you ought to get an hour?"

This, I knew, was my moment, so I straightened up in my chair, remembered the sixty mosquito bites, the hundred-and-five-degree heat, the endless hours, the dizziness, and the thirst, looked my father in the eye and said, "Seventy-five cents, Pop," which was not only twenty-five cents below the minimum wage, but four dollars and twenty-five cents below my pride, dignity, and sense of self-worth. Instantly, I thought of changing it to three dollars and seventy-five cents, but it was too late: my father had already nodded, and I had already smiled, and seventy-five cents an hour was my wage.

As my father turned to my brother to find out what he wanted per hour, I wondered what had gone wrong. Why, I wondered, had I only asked for seventy-five cents when I knew that I was worth five or six times that amount? Perhaps, I told myself, because I suddenly realized that to demand five times the minimum wage from a man who had provided me with food, shelter, clothing, and the best life had to offer was a shameless display of pettiness and ingratitude. Perhaps, at the very last moment, I realized that I should consider my three weeks of hard labor an honor instead of an outrage, and, in the spirit of gratitude and self-sacrifice, lowered my salary.

This did not quite explain why I lowered it to seventy-five cents instead of a dollar or a dollar fifty, but it did help me to enjoy the prime rib dinner we ate later that night, and to banish from my mind forever the notion that I had simply lost my nerve.

the ring

We had known Pop's ring for as long as we had
known Pop. It was made of gold with the carved figure
of a woman sitting among ruins, and a diamond in the
upper-right corner. We did not know who the woman
was or what the ruins or the diamond meant for many
years. All we knew was that we loved the ring and that
the ring was Pop as much as his smile or his voice or
his eyes or his laughter. When we played slap-hands
with him, the ring was there. When he tapped out a
rhythm on a drum or a tabletop for us to duplicate, the
ring was there. When all our arms fought against his
one arm in an arm-wrestling contest, the ring was
there.

The ring did not look like anything anyone could
purchase or purposely design. It seemed instead to
have just happened, as though all the good things my
father was had formed a gold ring around his finger
one night. Whatever it was about him that made us feel
safe was in the ring. Whatever it was about him that

made us love him, admire him, respect him, and fear him was in the ring. The ring was lightning in the sky and the taste of summer fruit. The ring was all the sweet sad music he had ever composed, along with his rage, his courage, his kindness, and his generosity. The ring was his face and the face of his soul forged in gold.

And maybe the qualities of the ring could be passed from one to another. Maybe the way he made us feel was the way we would make our own children feel. Maybe we were beginning to look a little more like him. Maybe we had his mouth, his eyes, his chin. And if we had his mouth, maybe we had his humor; and if we had his eyes, maybe we had his magnetism; and if we had his chin, maybe we had his strength.

Now and then he took the ring off for us to hold, and it was heavy and warm, and each of us felt as though we were holding something precious and substantial and magical. My father's hands were deeply tanned by the sun of vineyards, but the circle of flesh that the ring covered was white and soft and vulnerable looking. It reminded us, at least subliminally, who Pop was beneath his roar and his laughter. He was the soft white ring of flesh, but he was also the ring that covered it.

And then it was Christmas. My brother was twenty-two, and I was seventeen. We didn't know what the two small identically wrapped boxes were, but we knew they were special because Pop told us to save them for last. He sat behind us all morning, waiting. I had never seen him wait in this way before. I had seen him wait for Mom to put on her makeup; I had seen him wait in line for a movie; but I had never seen him wait like this. My mother and sister were waiting too. They knew what the gifts were and what they would mean.

When it came time to open the last two presents, my father told my brother and me to open them at the same time. So we picked up our separate boxes, untied the bows, took off the lids, removed the green sacks that contained the special thing, pulled open the puckered lips of the sacks, turned the sacks upside down, and felt the ring drop into each of our palms. For a moment time stopped, and then we looked at Pop.

life and times

Pop has not quite been himself. He seems gentler, more subdued, more at peace with himself and the world. One day he calls the family into his recording room to listen to his latest songs. He has been doing this for many years now. Sometimes we are not too crazy about the songs but say that we are. This time, however, is different. This time all the songs are good. This time all the songs are great. This time the songs are haunting, with superb lyrics and beautiful melodies. I am thrilled to finally be able to tell him how much I like his music.

One night at the dinner table, he looks at Mom and says to Carol, Skip, and me, "Look at that beautiful woman. Do you kids realize how lucky you are to have such a beautiful mother?"

One night, very late, I am talking to him about movies. He says that some of today's moviemakers are coasting. He says that it's not difficult to create images off the top of one's head. As an example, he gives me an image off the top of his head: A man, he says, is running on a hill while a clock ticks off the seconds. The man, he says, is running out of time:

over and out

You wake up and make yourself breakfast. You read the Sunday comics and eat with your brother and sister. It's ten o'clock. Your mother is in bed because she doesn't feel well. She has the flu. You mention to your brother and sister how nice it is that Pop is sleeping late. Usually he's downstairs before anyone. He must be pretty tired.

You wonder what you're going to do today. You may listen to music or ride your bike into town. You may even write a short story. You are a little worried about your mother. If anything ever happened to your mother, you would die of grief. Nothing will ever happen to your father, so you don't think about it. Last night you heard him walking around at one in the morning. You were sitting in the den watching television and his bedroom is above the den and you heard his footsteps on the ceiling. You thought to yourself, *Pop can't sleep.* Or maybe you felt sorry for him. Maybe you actually thought, *Poor Pop can't sleep. He must have a lot to think about.*

Now you are just finishing your breakfast. Your brother has gone outside to tan by the swimming pool. Your mother comes downstairs. You ask her how she is, and she says, better.

"Has Papa been down?" she asks.

"Not yet," you say. This, you think, is good news. It means he is sleeping and getting all the rest he needs.

Your mother does not look so happy. She tells you and your sister that Pop wasn't feeling well last night.

You remember Christmas Eve, twenty-three days ago, when you were not feeling well and he gave you hot tea with brandy and lemon and honey in it. You remember him tucking you into bed that night and making sure you were comfortable. And so you say, "I'm going to take him up some hot tea with brandy and honey and lemon juice."

But your mother says no—she's going to look in on him.

Why do you feel funny now? What has occurred to you, or almost occurred to you? You brush it aside and go upstairs to your room. You smile at your handsome reflection in the mirror. You brush your teeth. You look in the mirror again, and this time your expression changes. And then you feel funny again. Why? For some reason you get down on your knees and ask God to please not let your father die. You ask God to please not let him be dead. You feel a little funny praying for this because you know your father is fine.

Then you stand up. You feel better. You look in the mirror and smile at your handsome face again. No worry now. No funny feeling.

The phone rings. You answer it. It is Pam Green for your sister. You go into your sister's room and see your mother and sister talking. Neither of them looks quite right.

"Pam's on the phone," you say.

"Ask her if I can call her back," your sister says. Her voice is not too unlike her usual voice, yet you know something is wrong.

"What's going on?" you ask.

"Nothing," your sister says. Her voice is very gentle, but a little urgent too. You look at your mother, and she has a funny look on her face.

You ask Pam if Carol can call her back, and Pam says fine. You go to your bathroom, look at yourself in the mirror, and discover that you have the same funny look on your face that your mother had on hers. You get down on your knees and ask God please not to let your father be dead. This time you are praying for real. This time you sense that there really may be something wrong. You walk to your father's room and see that his door is closed. You go back to your room. You know all this has nothing to do with your father. You know you have a wild imagination and have blown something very small out of proportion. You know that your father is fine and that your mother and sister are talking about something else entirely. You have almost convinced yourself of this when your sister comes into your room and says that Mom wants to talk to you. Now you know that something is up.

"Is everything all right?" you ask.

"Oh, fine," your sister says. She says it very convincingly; she says it as though everything is really fine.

You go into your mother's room, and your mother is sitting on her bed. She still has that funny look on her face. It is sort of a dazed half smile.

"I have something to tell you," she says.

And now you know. You don't want to know, but you know anyway. It won't be real if she doesn't say it, but you know. There is nothing else that expression of hers can mean; there is nothing else her eyes can mean.

"Pop's dead," she says, and a white flash goes off in your head, and then you are crying faster than you have ever cried or smiled or winked or laughed or blinked in your life. And all at once you see everything—you see what it all means. It only takes an instant, but it's an eternal instant, an instant that would take years to write. And everything you feel is a forty-foot wave of water, and all at once you are in the wave, being tossed in the wave, and it's frightening because it's too strong. The wave can break you like a matchstick, and there are waves after this wave, higher and stronger, to break you apart and banish you to a vast unknown. And it shuts off and you are all right again. As fast as it started, it stops. And your eyes are dry and you are smiling. You think everything is all right again. You think you are over your father's death. You think you have stopped grieving.

You are seventeen, so you know you are right.

moving day

Time had come and gone. All the furniture was gone. All the books and paintings and silverware were gone. His mother and brother and sister were driving toward their separate homes, and in ten or twenty or thirty minutes he would leave this house for the last time. He was fully grown now—seven years older, five inches taller, and forty pounds heavier than the thirteen-year-old boy who had been beaten up by Mike Dichter so many Mondays ago. He had a muscular frame, sideburns, hair on his chest, a green belt in karate, and the sad awareness that he would never see his family within these walls again.

The unpolished wood of the entry hall was scuffed and scratched where the moving men had slid the packed boxes and wheeled the piano and TVs out the door. Through the window he could see the untrimmed tops of the hedges, the little clumps of yellowing weeds and patches of burnt grass in the once-immaculate lawn. He noticed all the leaves on the patio and wondered what his father would say about it. He wondered how he would explain to him that he didn't sweep it anymore.

With echoing footsteps he walked across the hall and entered the empty oval of the breakfast room. He glanced at the small mound under the worn yellow carpet, remembering the first time his mother's foot pressed down upon it and hearing the buzzer that sounded in the kitchen as clearly as he had heard it that day. As hard as he tried, he could not really believe that this was the room where his mother had been so young, his sister a teenager, his brother a ten-year-old boy with braces on his teeth. The unreality of the room made him feel unreal as well, and if, at that moment, anyone had entered, he was sure they would not have seen him, any more than they would have seen the chairs where his family once sat, the table where they had eaten, the polished floors and spotless carpets. They would walk right through him on their way into the living room to measure the walls, or up to his mother's room to measure her closets. He looked out the window at the anonymous backyard where, seemingly, no party had ever been, no band had ever played, no couple had ever danced, and walked out of the empty room to the foot of the green carpeted staircase.

He looked up at the chandelier, remembering the first time he had seen it. On the smudged white wall to his right was the light switch that lit the white candles, and he turned it on and off, on and off, as he had fourteen years earlier. He tried to feel the same wonder he had felt then, but there was no magic left in the lit candles and reflecting crystals. He ran his hand over the chipped and dusty banister and looked up at the stairway that had once beckoned him to one mystery and now beckoned him to another. He climbed the stairs slowly, for his heart was beating too fast and he had the unpleasant sensation of floating in a dream.

When he reached the landing, he took his pulse, a habit he'd picked up after his father died, and felt a rapid throbbing against his first two fingers. He took a deep breath to calm himself and stepped into his sister's room. He hardly saw it. All he could feel was his heart beating. It was the same when he went to his mother's room, then his father's.

He stood in the middle of his own room now, as empty feeling and anonymous as all the others. He looked at the built-in shelves where his books had been, the indentations in the brown carpet where his desk had been. Through the window he could see the faraway trees in his neighbor's backyard, and beyond them the enchanted visions of his childhood—the magic carpets of Arabia, the bullrings of Spain, and the oceans where the sirens sang.

He went into the bathroom, looked in the mirror, and saw the last of his faces he would ever see there. And all he wanted to do now was go back to the beginning, to the first face, to the tree in the front yard that couldn't be climbed, to hanging clothes in the new closets with his brother. But it was someone else's room now. He had come to say goodbye to it, but it was already gone, as far away as his father.

He walked to the doorway, took a last look at the beds where he and his brother slept, said goodbye to the two boys who had slept there, and walked down the back stairs, through the breakfast room, across the faded wooden floor of the entry hall, to the front door. He hesitated there, knowing it was time to leave. He wondered what he would do tomorrow, and all the days after that. He did not know how any one of those days could resolve itself into a life or a career or a wife or a family. All he knew for certain was that he could no longer stay here, and that a new family was going to polish these floors, paint these walls, furnish these rooms, and make them their own.

He looked around the hall for the last time, then at the green staircase. He remembered his six-year-old self seeing those stairs for the first time. He remembered how they seemed to recede to an unknown that frightened him, a faraway future where bicycles rusted in garages, love notes yellowed in basement boxes, and all the surfaces of all the swimming pools were as clear and cold as glass. He had always known, somewhere inside him, that that future was coming.

And here he was standing in the center of it, facing a new unknown, another new house waiting to be made into a home.

epilogue

the water pump

I was standing under a tree in Fresno thinking about painting the belly of a water pump white. It wasn't a very big water pump, and I had been painting it for ten minutes, but I couldn't make myself lie on my back and paint its belly. I couldn't because I was afraid of spiders, and Fresno, I knew, was black widow country. I had been afraid of spiders ever since I was four years old and my baby-sitter had shrieked and pointed in a corner three feet behind my bed and said, "There's a spider. It can kill you!" From that moment on, whenever I saw a spider, my heart and body leaped back two or three literal and figurative feet in terror. I certainly would have finished the job if I had been in another part of the country—say, Connecticut—but this was Fresno, and I wasn't about to challenge death for a water pump.

Then again, I did have a job to do, and my father had been after me to complete things for years. He had been after me to finish drying the hubcaps after I washed them, and to sweep the leaves out of the corners of the patio, and to just generally be the best person I could be. I wanted to be the best person I could be too, but I didn't want to die doing it. Anyway, I had been finishing what I started since I had come to the vineyard twelve days before.

Then again, it was hard to look at that lovely white water pump and know that it had a dirty brown belly. It meant that I hadn't finished the job. It meant that I was the same person I had been a year ago, two years ago. What did my father want from me? Did he want me to die? I agreed with him that I was lazy and half-assed, but surely this was not the time to start completing things. And who was going to know that the underside of the water pump hadn't been painted? And who would care? Anyway, my father was in Los Angeles and I was in Fresno, so he would never know.

Then again, I didn't really want to be lazy and half-assed, so I summoned all the bravery and determination I had, slid under the water pump, tried with all my might to ignore the threat of spiders, failed, panicked, and got to my feet.

I couldn't do it. There was no shame in that. No shame at all. I would have finished painting the water pump if I hadn't been in Fresno and God hadn't invented black widows. So I walked away from the water pump, feeling I had done my best, and went to join my brother, who was scraping paint off the bunkhouse windows.

Twenty-five minutes later we saw my father's Mercedes driving toward the bunkhouse for a surprise visit. I was happy to see him because I truly believed that I had become a more industrious, hardworking human being, and I couldn't wait for him to see the new me—the me that had walked up and down countless rows of vines under a blazing sun, uprooted weeds, turned canes, painted fences, and developed muscles. Also, I had forgotten all about the water pump.

After Skip and I hugged and kissed him, he asked us how we were.

"Great," we said.

"Working hard?"

"Real hard."

Ten minutes later we were taking him on a tour of his vineyard and showing him the wondrous improvements our hard work had wrought. He seemed pleased and proud and happy, and I knew that at least half of his pleasure, pride, and happiness had to do with me.

Then we came to the water pump, and I remembered everything. For a moment I thought there was a chance that my father might concentrate on the joy of being on his own vineyard with his own two sons and not look under the water pump. But my father was born to notice everything, especially unfinished jobs.

"What kind of a half-assed job is this?" he said, looking under the water pump.

There was no way to answer that question, so I remained silent.

"Who painted this?"

"I did," I said.

"Look at the bottom here."

I looked.

"You call this finished?"

"No," I said. I didn't even consider telling him about my fear of spiders and the possibility of death. All I could do was stare at the brown rusty unpainted belly of the water pump.

My father shook his head, as though words had not been invented to describe his disgust and disappointment. "Just finish it," he said.

After he left I lay down on my back and finished painting the water pump, complaining to myself all the while about certain men who were always finding fault with their sons. Looking back, however, I realize that if he had been the kind of man who always allowed himself the luxury of enjoying the company of his sons, the sight and smell of his vineyard, and three-quarters of a water pump, I would never have finished this book.